Eilis

His Ladies with the Lamps
Book 4

By

Ronna M. Bacon

The Ladies with the Lamps

Matthew 25: 6-10

6 "And at midnight a cry was heard: 'Behold, the bridegroom is coming; go out to meet him!' 7 Then all those virgins arose and trimmed their lamps. 8 And the foolish said to the wise, 'Give us some of your oil, for our lamps are going out.' 9 But the wise answered, saying, 'No, lest there should not be enough for us and you; but go rather to those who sell, and buy for yourselves.' 10 And while they went to buy, the bridegroom came, and those who were ready went in with him to the wedding; and the door was shut.

Eilis

Psalms 46:1

God is our refuge and strength, an ever-present help in time of trouble.

Psalm 57:1

Have mercy on me, my God, have mercy on me, for in you I take refuge. I will take refuge in the shadow of your wings until the disaster has passed.

NKJV

Table of Contents

Wandering through a nearby town, Eilis Whitman was very uneasy. She had escaped from her town to be by herself, or at least she hoped that she had. She looked around the little store that she had just discovered, her eyes taking in the beautiful handcrafts that were for sale. Eilis was feeling followed and kept searching for whoever that was. And she did not like that one bit.

She strode from the building, not purchasing the rainbow that she had been touching. She just wasn't in the mood for that. Standing on the sidewalk for a moment, Eilis finally sighed to herself. She had not been herself for months now, not since her cousins, Brinn and Darbi, and her own sister, Chani, had gone through what they termed as their adventures. That was a given, she thought.

Shaking her head, Eilis moved to a street vendor, purchasing a coffee and a muffin. She looked around, finally heading for the little park the vendor had pointed to. He grinned at her, wondering that a beautiful lady like her was on her own.

Tugging at the dark brown curls caught back into a ponytail, her brown eyes assessing those around her. She smiled at the small children running and playing around her. She missed being that little, out with her sister and mother and usually her two cousins and her aunt.

Eilis looked around. She was still feeling eyes on her and didn't like it one bit. She could not see anyone who was watching her. She sighed to herself. No, she didn't want an adventure such as her family had had. Not at all.

The man watching her moved closer. He had orders to find Eilis Whitman and bring her to his employer. Failure to do that was not acceptable. His eyes raised, as had Eilis', to study the people in the park. He didn't see anyone that concerned him and his feet took him closer to the young lady. He paused as he watched a younger man hesitate and then sit by Eilis, drawing her into a conversation.

Declan Sullivan had decided to take a break himself that day and wander through this town. He was restless, needing to find something new to do. He watched the young lady wander the town ahead of him and also saw the older man who was following her. He didn't like that at all. Declan sighed. No, it wasn't up to him to intervene. His auburn hair moved in the slight breeze as he turned away, his green eyes thoughtful.

A sudden decision on his part had him heading for the same vendor, a coffee in his hand as he turned. He walked the same path that Eilis had, his steps slowing as he neared. A sudden impulse had him brushing past the man and then sitting beside her, his coffee raised to drink from.

Eilis had jumped as she heard someone sit beside her. She twisted slightly to stare at the young man, a frown on her face. She looked up to see herself indeed being watched. Eilis looked around, trying to find a path to escape on but not seeing one.

"I'm sorry to scare you." Declan spoke, his eyes on the man, his voice barely audible. "You're being watched. I would like to help you."

Eilis stared at him for a moment before her eyes narrowed. *Is this You, God? Have You provided some way for me to get out of here? I know that You can do this. I'm just not sure that You have. I need a sign to accept this.*

Declan could feel Eilis staring at him but he refused to look away from the man. The man, heavy set and older than him by a number of years, had stopped moving towards Eilis, anger on his face directed towards Declan.

"I'm sorry. I don't know you. I don't know why you would say that." Eilis turned back around, her eyes on the man in front of her. She grew afraid, more afraid than she had ever been. She could feel the evil from him, evil directed towards her. Only, she had no idea why that was.

"No, you don't. My name is Declan Sullivan. I wasn't intending on intruding. But that gentleman over there seems to mean you harm. And it is not in me to let any harm come to a lady, let alone as beautiful a young lady as you are."

Eilis stared at him, shock on her face before she frowned.

"Excuse me? Do you always say that to people?" She went to rise, finding his hand on her arm keeping her on the Davidch. "Your hand?"

"No, I don't usually do this. But I just sense such a presence of evil directed towards you. And from that man who seems very interested in you." Declan nodded towards him. "It's not in me to let any harm come to you. It's not how I was raised."

"I see." Eilis bit at her lip, not sure how to respond. "I'm Eilis Whitman. To tell you the truth, I have felt followed. I'm not from this town and didn't know where to turn or who to turn to for help."

"It's not my town either. I'm from another town." When he named it, she stared at him. "Is that a problem?"

"No, that's my town. At least it has been since I was nine and came to live with my aunt." She blew out a breath. "So, what now? I can't see getting by him."

"I'm not sure that we can." Declan dumped his coffee cup into the trash, reaching for her garbage and doing the same. He leaned forward to look at her feet. Good, he thought, she's wearing sneakers. That helps. If we can get around him, then we can literally make a run for it.

"How are you at running?" Declan grinned at her, trying to give the impression that they were friends. And he suddenly wanted that, very much. He didn't want Eilis to walk out of his life and never be seen again.

"I'm decent at it." Eilis studied him and then the man. "We're making a run for it? But where do we head?"

"Away from here." Declan was on his feet, Eilis' hand tight in his, as he ran for the opposite side of the park. He was somewhat familiar with it, knowing that they could circle around to find their vehicles.

Eilis' fleeing feet kept pace with him, her breath coming in gasps. Declan slid to a halt near his vehicle.

"Where are you parked?" He looked around, seeing that they seemed to have escaped the man for the moment.

"At another parking lot. I need to get there." Eilis looked up with shock as Declan simply unlocked his truck and shoved her inside, the door slamming after her before he ran for the driver's side.

Declan drove away as rapidly as he could, his eyes seeing the man appearing in the rearview mirror, a phone in his hand. His heart sank. They had gotten away from him but there must be someone else out there. He slowed as Eilis pointed out her car.

"This isn't good." Eilis' face whitened as her heart fell. "There's someone there."

"There is." Declan kept on going, looking for help. He pulled to the side of the road. "I can get someone here to tow it to your home. I'll drive you there, if you're comfortable enough to do that."

Eilis studied him, knowing that he was putting himself out there, putting himself between herself and the men who seemed determined to take her with them.

"I guess. This is not how I planned my day." She sounded disgruntled.

"It never is." Declan made a quick call. "My friend will meet us here."

"I can't let you put yourself at risk. I'll find a ride home." Eilis stared out of the side window, missing the look that Declan gave her.

"Not a problem, Eilis. You know, I think I've seen you at church. You have three or four sisters that you're usually with?"

Eilis turned, a frown on her face. She didn't remember seeing him

"No, just one sister, two cousins, and an aunt. Aunt Ashlynn raised us when our parents were all murdered." Eilis drew in a deep breath, ready to continue but her words turned to a scream as she saw the truck heading for them. Her scream split the air in the cab before it died away. The heavy sounds of metal crumpling and alarms sounding rang through the air as the heavy truck backed up and moved away. The couple lay motionless as bystanders stared in horror before men were running towards the truck, trying to access the cab. Red and blue emergency lights flashed through the mid-afternoon light, bringing aid to the couple.

Patrol officers searched for answers, finding none. Incidents like this didn't happen in a town called Mistletoe. At least not this type. The authorities worked quickly to stabilize the couple for transport. Sirens sounded as they were rushed away, leaving unanswered questions amid the debris of Declan's truck. This was not how the day was to end.

—

The man watched in horror as the truck had crashed into Declan's truck. His accomplice had been on his way towards him when the crash had happened. They shared a look before they turned and ran for a car, intent on heading to the hospital. There was still a chance that there would be an opportunity to take Eilis and disappear with her.

Chapter 2

Ashlynn Whitman dropped her phone on her lap, horror on her face as she reached to bury it in her hands. An arm around her caused her to jump as she looked up at Chani, one of her nieces. Chani, Brinn, and Darbi had dropped in that morning, just to spend some time with her. Their husbands, Ronan, Gareth, and Flynn were out for breakfast themselves.

"Aunt Ash? You have gone white?" Chani's shared a look with her cousins. "What happened?"

"It's Eilis."

"Yes, where is Eilis? She's not here?" Brinn was a little put out at her cousin, knowing that they usually met all together. "Where is she?"

"She just said that she needed to get away for a day. By herself. She's been working through what we all went through and wondering if she is going to be next." Darbi reached to hug her aunt. "But that doesn't explain the phone call Aunt Ash just got."

Ashlynn shook her head, her eyes finding her nieces.

"It was a police officer from Mistletoe. Eilis is in the hospital there. Some kind of accident. But she wasn't alone, he said. There was a man with her." She looked around. "Is Eilis dating someone and hasn't told us?"

"No, she's not." Chani was adamant about that. "I would know."

—

Ashlynn was on her feet, hearing the men's voices as they entered her home. They looked at her, frowns on their faces.

"Aunt Ash?" Gareth reached out a hand to stop her forward walk. "Something has happened."

"It is. Eilis has been in an accident. I need to get to Mistletoe. Thank goodness that's not too far away."

The men exchanged glances with themselves and then their wives.

"It's okay. We'll drive. Let's get ourselves sorted out. If we car pool, that would be better."

Chani turned her head to watch her aunt, a frown on her face. *What had happened to her little sister? I pray that she's okay, Lord. I couldn't handle it if she is hurt really bad. Now I know how the others felt to some extent.*

Ronan turned his head enough to glance at Chani.

"Chani, what do we know?"

"Not a lot." Her voice was as low as his. "All we know is that Eilis was in an accident. I don't know if she was given much more than that." She twisted in her seat to look at her aunt once more.

Ashlynn headed for the clerk in the emergency ward before she returned to her nieces, almost frantic with worry. She simply hugged her nieces, huge their husbands, and then sat, her eyes on the door, not sure where to go or what to do. Her heart raised in prayer for Eilis.

—

Ronan paced with Gareth and Flynn, his eyes on his wife and her aunt. This was not what they had expected that day. Not at all.

"Why was Eilis here?" Flynn finally broke their silence.

Gareth shrugged, his eyes on Brinn.

"Chani told Brinn that Eilis hadn't been herself the last week or two. She refused to meet with them today, simply saying that she had plans out of town." Gareth paused his words, a frown wrinkling his brow. "I don't know what would have brought her to Mistletoe."

"Likely just to go to another town to be by herself." Flynn had talked it over with Darbi early that morning when she told him about Eilis. "Things have changed for her with the three married. She's feeling left out, no doubt."

"Their relationships have changed. It is only natural." Gareth agreed, turning as he heard footsteps near him. A nurse had appeared and approached Ashlynn.

Ashlynn was on her feet, Chani's hand in hers as she nodded and then followed the nurse. The other two ladies found their fellows, standing with them, their fellows' arms around them. They were worried, not knowing what was going on.

Gareth simply prayed for Eilis before the other two men did as well.

"Didn't Ashlynn say a man was involved?" Brinn was puzzled. Eilis was not dating.

—

"She did? I didn't hear that." Flynn looked around as he heard the door opening and closing and an older couple made their way inside. "Say. Isn't that David and Angela Sullivan from church?"

"It is." Darbi paled. "Was Declan with Eilis? I didn't know that they knew one another."

"I didn't think that they did." Ronan walked away, heading for the Sullivans who had turned, worry and uncertainty on their faces. "David?"

"Ronan?" David stopped his steps, looking past him at the others. "You're all here? Who's hurt?"

"Eilis was." Ronan paused, a thought halting his word. "David? Is Declan here?"

"He is." David turned as he felt Angela's hand on his back. "Angela?"

"They said that he was with a young lady. Was it Eilis? We know her from around church."

"It might be. We were told that she was a man." Ronan paused, turning to face the doors again.

"I didn't think that they knew one another." Angela wrapped her arm around David. "Do they?"

"Come and sit with us." Ronan pointed to where the others were. "Ashlynn and Chani are back with Eilis."

"How serious is she?" Angela was afraid to ask.

"We don't yet." Flynn reached to shake their hands. "We haven't been told yet. But I don't understand why you are here."

"Declan was injured." David looked around. "We think that he and Eilis were together for some reason."

This shocked Eilis' family. She hadn't been dating, not that they were aware of. So how did this happen? All any of them could do was pray for healing for them and protection from the gathering storm that was dropping down on the couple.

Chapter 3

Ashlynn turned from the stretcher before her eyes turned back to her youngest niece. Eilis had always needed that extra hug from her aunt. Losing her parents when she was just nine had been difficult. Ashlynn had tried to step in but she knew that it wasn't the same.

Eilis watched through partially opened eyelids as her aunt and sister moved away. She hurt but she was thankful that she was alive. She just didn't know the ladies who had just left. She felt like she should.

Sighing, she swung her feet over the edge of the bed and waited. She had been lucky, she was told, that she ended up with only a concussion and bumps and bruises. The truck had taken the brunt of the hit. She just wanted to find the man that she had been with. *Declan,* she thought, *his name was. She could remember him. He had tried to protect her. Lord, where is he? Is he still alive? And why can't I remember what went on before the accident? Isn't it usually the other way around?*

Sneaking from her room, Eilis hesitated for a moment. She could hear a man's voice and walked that way, standing just outside the room door. She watched as Declan sat on the stretcher, a sling around his left arm. She drew in a deep breath. Declan had been injured because of her. That she didn't know if she could live with.

Declan looked up at a slight noise, seeing movement outside his door. His hand reached out for Eilis who almost ran towards him. His hand clasped hers tightly even as he turned back to the physician who was speaking with him.

The physician eyed the couple before he nodded. More than friends, he thought. They'll need one another to get past the trauma that they suffered today.

"So, Declan, you'll need to rest that shoulder for about a week. Keep it in the sling for a couple of days. We need you to start moving the shoulder as much as you can even then. Any other questions?" When Declan shook his head, the physician turned to Eilis.

"And you, young lady. You have a concussion, you know. You need to rest. No working for at least a week." He handed them their discharge paperwork and walked away.

"Declan? Your shoulder?" Eilis' voice was barely above a whisper.

"It's okay. It's really bruised. That's all." His hand reached out to touch the bruise on her cheek. "A concussion?"

Eilis nodded, a frown on her face that turned to a troubled look.

"I have a huge problem." Her voice died away as she fought the fear rising within her.

"And that would be." Declan waited patiently, knowing somehow that their lives were now entwined in something that neither of them had wanted or planned.

—

"There was a lady here and a younger lady. They said that they were my aunt and sister." Eilis blinked away the tears that had clouded her vision. "Only, I don't remember them. Shouldn't I if we're related?"

Declan stared at her, his eyes raising to the physician who had hesitated outside of the door before he came in. The physician studied Eilis for a moment before he spoke, causing her to jump.

"Eilis? What was that you just said?"

She turned to him, a frown puckering her forehead as she struggled to understand what had happened.

"I can remember Declan. I can't remember those two ladies. They said they're family but I don't recognize them." She swiped at the tears on her face. "And I can't remember much before this morning."

The physician nodded. He had seen something like this when he first started practicing. That person never did regain their memory, devastating a family.

"It's entirely possible. Trauma does funny things to us. And so do concussions. I would suggest that you rest for a few days. Don't push trying to remember. That will come when you least expect, I suspect." He spoke to her for a few more moments before he walked away.

"Declan? How are you to get home? Your truck? And we sent my car back to my place already so I can't drive you."

Declan's finger lightly touched her lips, silencing her words.

—

"It's okay. Mom and Dad are here. They'll give us a lift. But your family is all out there. Your aunt, your sister and her husband, your two cousins and their husbands. They will expect you to go with them."

"I can't. I just can't." Eilis whirled around and ran from him, out of the doors where an ambulance was waiting to offload a stretcher.

Declan simply handed his father their paperwork and was after her, finding her standing in the parking lot. *She looked lost, alone, worried but oh so beautiful,* he thought. *I can't let anyone hurt her, not even her family. But how do I do that, Lord? We'll go home and go our separate ways. Only I don't want to do that.*

David stopped beside his son, his eyes questioning although he didn't ask those questions.

"Dad? We have a huge problem." Declan didn't know how to continue. He prayed for the words that he needed.

"And that would be, son?"

"Eilis doesn't remember anything before today. She remembers me. She just doesn't remember her family. And she is refusing to go with them." Declan drew in a deep breath. "How do we do this? They will expect her to go with them."

"I know that they will. We know Ashlynn from church. You've been in and out for so many years that you haven't connected with the younger folks. Let me talk to Ashlynn and see what we do. Take her to my truck. We'll meet you there." David handed over his

---

keys, watching as Declan approached Eilis and then, with an arm around her, led her to David's vehicle. He shook his head, his face raising for a moment as he prayed for his son and the lady who seemed to have caught his attention.

David walked slowly back into the waiting room, finding Angela watching for him. He hugged her, a few low words in her ear, before he turned to find Ashlynn. Ashlynn still had her focus on the doors, not hearing David come to sit beside her.

"Ashlynn?" David waited for Ashlynn to turn to him. He could see the rest of the family gathered close to them. "Ashlynn, we need to talk."

"David? What is it? Eilis should be released soon." Her eyes moved between David and the doors.

"She's been released already. But there is a problem." He hesitated, not quite sure how to continue. "She found Declan and they're together. But like I said, there is a huge problem. When she found Declan, she told him that she can't remember anything before today."

Ashlynn stared at him, hearing the surprise and the worried murmurs from her family.

"What was that?" Ashlynn wasn't sure that she had heard him correctly.

"She doesn't remember you or Chani. She told Declan that. When she ran, he went after her. They're at my truck right now."

"She can't remember us?" Chani sank to the floor beside her aunt, her hand on Ashlynn's. "Is that even possible?"

"I have no idea. But something has happened to block you from her memory. We'll work with her. Today? Can you let her have today? She has her phone, doesn't she? Send her text messages that you love her and want to see her but that you understand. She needs the reinforcement of your love and the choice to make her decisions."

Ashlynn nodded, her eyes on her family. She could see the shock on their faces, the same look that she was sure on hers.

"God is in control, David. We will do that. Tell her that we love her and we want to be with her. We can't understand what she is going through. None of us have been through that. Tell her that we want her home." Ashlynn buried her face in her hands, feeling Chani's arms around her and the younger lady's tears on her face.

Chapter 4

Her hand tight in Declan's, Eilis stared at the apartment building. She had been told that it was her home. Only, she didn't recognize it. Declan watched her before he shared a look with his father. This was not how he planned to end his day, that was a given.

"Eilis? Here. Let's get you out. You can stay with Mom and Dad if you feel better doing that." Declan waited patiently for her to make her move.

Eilis walked towards her home, as she was told it was, her hand tight in Declan's. She knew that was not something that she did, hold a man's hand. But he made her feel safe and cherished. Today, that was what she needed.

Declan unlocked her door, shoving it open, and waiting for her to move inside. He tilted his head to look at her before he looked at his parents. Angela moved in on Eilis, an arm around her, walking her in.

David watched as his son drew in a deep breath. This was not easy, he knew.

"Son? Where will she go? I had a chance to speak with Ashlynn. They were shocked but still want to be with her."

"Of course, they would. That's what family does." Declan turned back to the door. "She can stay with you and Mom?"

"Of course she can. And you are as well. Just for tonight at least, Declan. Mom will want to mother

---

you." He grinned at his son, finding him smiling back. "Let's see what your lady wants to do and where she wants to be. Although I suspect that she wants to be where you are."

Declan stared at his father's back before he nodded. His father's words had surprised him but he knew that he didn't want Eilis to walk away from him. Not ever. And that was not how he was.

Eilis looked around her bedroom as she zippered closed a bag. She had packed enough for a few days, knowing that she would not be back for a while. She sighed. That lady from the hospital? She did look familiar but she just wasn't sure. Walking to her dresser, Eilis picked up a framed photo of the two ladies, herself, and two other ladies around her own age. She sighed once more, knowing that was likely true, that they were family. Otherwise, she would not have that photo.

Angela had stood back watching Eilis before she moved in on her, an arm around her. She prayed for her young friend, knowing that this was difficult for her.

"You can stay with us, Eilis. Now, let's get home with you. What about your work? Do you remember that?"

Eilis shook her head, not remembering where she worked or what she even did.

"No, I don't. There might be information in the other room." Eilis headed that way, leaving Declan to stare after before he took the bag from his mother.

<hr>

"Mom?"

"She's trying to find out where she works."

Declan paled at that.

"She wouldn't remember, now would she?" He turned, torn about where he needed to be. He handed the bag to his father and headed after her.

Eilis stood for a moment, her hands on a folder. This would give her a window into her life. Only she wasn't sure if she wanted that. She felt hands on her shoulders and then Declan praying for her. She leaned back against him for a moment.

"This is your work info?" Declan's voice was low as he spoke.

"I think so." Eilis opened the folder, staring down at the paystub. "It says that I work for a florist. Only I don't remember that. I need to call her."

"We can do that. I think Mom and Dad know her."

"No, I need to do that. This affects so many people. Do we even know why?"

"No, we don't. The patrol officer who I spoke with said that he would be in touch. Now, do you have everything that you need?'

Eilis nodded and turned, finding her nose hitting Declan's chest. He simply hugged her, his chin resting on the top of her head, before he turned, his hand finding hers. He walked towards his mother, finding her eyes on him and then Eilis.

—

"Eilis works for Sally at her shop. We'll need to call them."

Eilis glared at him for a moment.

"I said that I would."

"And you can. We'll be there if you need us. That's all." Angela shook her head at her son, knowing that he wanted to step in and make it all better for the young lady but he couldn't. He didn't have the right to do that.

Eilis sighed, her head beginning to pound. She reached for her phone, dialling the number on the paystub. She spoke quietly, not giving much information other than that she had been in a car accident and had to be off work. She had a sick note for that.

She turned away from the phone, laying it down and staring at it. She watched as Declan reached for it, tucking it into his pocket and then reaching for her hand.

David and Angela watched the young couple on the way to their home. Neither was sure what was happening, but something was. They could feel the danger approaching their son, without knowing who or why. That it was connected to Eilis, that was the only thing that they were sure of. They were just as sure that Declan would not walk away from Eilis, not if he could help it.

Ashlynn paced her home, arms wrapped around herself. She was troubled, more so than she had been with the others. At least, those girls had not hid themselves from the others. That was what she felt Eilis was doing.

Chani approached her, handing over a mug of coffee. She could hear Ronan moving around in the kitchen, just letting her have time with her aunt.

"Aunt Ashlynn? Is that true?"

"What true?" Ashlynn turned to study Chani, seeing the stress on her face. "That Eilis can't remember us? It is possible. I've just never heard of it quite this way."

"So, what do we do? How do we help her?" Chani leaned back against Ronan as he wrapped her into his arms.

"We wait, sweetheart." Ronan made her sit, an arm around her. "We can't force it. That never works. All we can do is pray for her and be there when she needs us."

Chani sighed, her eyes on Ashlynn.

"That's all we can do, but I don't like it."

"It doesn't matter if we like it or not. We can't take over her life. She will make her decisions. All we can do is pray for her."

Ronan sat silent for a moment.

"I just don't understand the accident. I talked to David. He said that they were just sitting there when the truck rammed them. I didn't know that Declan and Eilis knew one another."

"They didn't." Chani was puzzled by that as well.

Chapter 5

Eilis paced the yard at David and Angela's, her jacket pulled up around her neck. The early morning was cold but she refused to go into the house. She didn't know where to go. All she knew was that she was fighting the worse headache of her life. Jumping as she sensed someone near her, she felt Declan's hand grasping her. She clung to him, knowing that he was her lifeline right now.

"Are you okay?" Declan's voice broke through the silence.

Eilis shook her head and then regretted it. The headache began to pound. She gave a sigh as Declan swept her into his arms and headed for the house, ignoring the sharp pain from his shoulder. He set her down in the kitchen and pulled out a chair, making her sit.

"Declan? What is going on?" His mother's voice came from behind him.

"Her headache. That's what happened." Declan could feel himself growing angry and knew that he needed to release that. "Who did this? Do we even know?"

"I spoke with the investigator last night." David reached to hug his son, shoving him down in turn in a chair. "There is no information that he has that would tell us who. There were no security systems where you had parked."

"I see." Declan rubbed at his shoulder, his eyes on Eilis.

Eilis turned to him, a tortured look coming to her face.

"Declan? Can I go home? I need to do that." Her head became buried on her folded arms as she wept.

Declan simply wrapped an arm around her and his head Davidt near hers as he prayed for her.

Angela shared a look with David before she nodded. They would not be at church that morning. She simply rose and went to find her phone. Eilis needed her aunt whether she knew who she was or not and she needed her sister.

Ashlynn turned from her door, looking at Chani as she stood watching her aunt. Chani had stopped by, just hoping that Eilis had come home.

"Aunt Ash?"

Ashlynn looked up at her, a sad smile on her face.

"Angela called. She has asked if we could meet at their place. Eilis needs us, even if she doesn't remember us."

Chani hugged her aunt, her eyes on Ronan.

"We can do that. Brinn and Darbi?"

"Just us for now. We'll see how she is when we get there." Ashlynn listened as Ronan prayed for them. She reached for her phone when he finished, simply sending a text to Brinn and Chani and asking for their prayers.

Angela stood back from the door, watching as the three entered. Declan had managed to calm Eilis down and had her in the office, trying to help her remember her life. That was going about as well as Angela had expected it to. She knew her son, though, and that he would not give up on finding the answers.

"Angela? How is she?" Ashlynn stood for a moment, looking for Eilis.

"She's hurting, Ashlynn. The headache is bad and she's not taking anything for it."

Chani gave a low laugh.

"That's Eilis. She won't take pain medications. She never has, even when she really needs to." Chani looked around. "Can we find her?"

"You can. Follow that hallway and she's in the office. I told her that you were on your way. She didn't respond."

Chani stood in the hallway, Ronan's arm around her, just watching her sister. She moved to sit near her, not saying a word. She could tell that Eilis knew that she was there but was refusing to look up.

Declan sighed. This was not what was to be happening. This was not how he planned his day. But Eilis came first. That was a given.

"Declan, is it?" Ronan reached to shake his hand before he sat near his wife. His eyes flickered between the sisters, not sure what he should say. "What

—

happened yesterday? We just were told that you two were in an accident."

Declan nodded, his eyes on Eilis.

"There's not a lot to tell. I followed Eilis in Mistletoe. We hadn't met there. I was watching her being followed and went up to her and offered to help her. We had managed to get to my truck and made arrangements to have her car towed back here by a friend of mine. While we were just sitting there, a truck rammed us. I didn't have a chance to move."

Eilis had turned her head to watch Chani as Declan spoke. She frowned for a moment, a scene tickling at her memory.

"Chani? What happened? Where am I?" Eilis turned as she felt a hand on hers. She jumped before she simply found herself wrapped in Declan's arms.

"You're safe. You're with friends." Chani blinked to clear her eyes.

"I am?" Eilis looked up at Declan. "Declan? Did we know that man?"

"No, I don't think that we do. He was following you. That's why I sat beside you. I did not want you to face him on your own."

Eilis watched as Ashlynn appeared, sitting near her but letting her have her space. *That was her aunt,* she thought.

She's been like that all her life, Ashlynn thought. *She needs space to think through things before she will talk. That's what we give her.*

—

Eilis sat, watching her family, content to be held. Ashlynn frowned for a moment once more, knowing that this was not Eilis. But then, with what she went through and Declan there at the time, it was to be expected. She simply prayed for her niece and her friend, knowing that if Eilis followed the others' examples, she had just found the knight woven into her stories.

Angela watched her son, exchanging a glance with David. They both knew that this was not Declan to act like this. He was always so careful in how he approached the ladies. He would never sit like this. They could see the contentment on his face, the knowledge that he had not yet acknowledged to himself that he had found his lady.

Chapter 6

Eilis had returned to her apartment but felt uneasy there. Something was off in it. Only she had no idea just what it was. Declan had stayed after the others had left, his eyes on her. He walked towards her, stopping her with his hands on her shoulders.

"Something's off?"

Eilis nodded.

"There is and I don't know what." She sighed as the doorbell rang. "I don't need anyone else here other than you." She walked away from him.

Declan stared at her and then headed for the door. He pulled it open to find Frank, a friend but also a police investigator, standing there.

"Frank?" He motioned him in.

"Declan? You're here? I heard what happened. Where's Eilis?" Frank stepped out of his shoes and hung up his jacket. He was there as an investigator that day, not just as a friend.

"I am. I brought Eilis home from Mom and Dad's. We stayed there last night. Her family left not that long enough. She's feeling very overwhelmed as well as fighting a headache and pain."

"And she'll refuse to take anything. But there's more?" Frank's keen eyes assessed the younger man.

"There is. Eilis feels something off in here. She had just mentioned it when you appeared." Declan was watching past Frank, seeing Eilis standing there. "Eilis?"

Frank turned, assessing his young friend before he nodded. *She's hurting and in so many ways. I prayed that she would avoid what the other ladies did, but it doesn't look as if that will happen. Help us, Lord, to protect her.*

"Eilis? Glad you're home. But what's this I hear? Something's off in here?"

"There is, Frank. I'm glad that you are here. I need this to be over. I don't want to go through what the others did. And I certainly don't need you hurt on my behalf. Where's Adam?"

"Adam? He's away on vacation. He hasn't taken one for a year and was told that he had to. He's glad to be away. He needs it." Frank looked around, liking the fact that Eilis kept her apartment tidy and didn't have a lot of knick knacks around. "How be I take a look around and see what I can find? And yes, Abe will send Joseph if he needs to. You know that."

Declan frowned at that. He didn't know an Abe, at least he didn't think that he did. Eilis watched him and then reached for his hand, pulling him to the kitchen. She had an eye on the clock, as best she could see through the pain that she was in.

"Sit, Eilis. If you'll let me, I'll fix you something to eat."

"I have sandwich stuff in the fridge." She sighed as she sat, reluctantly taking the medication bottle and the glass of water that he handed her. "Yes, mother.

———

I'll take these. I don't know if I've ever had such a headache."

"It will ease but for now, take your medications if you need to."

"I will. Frank? What did you find or not find?" Eilis squinted at him as he grinned at her.

Frank knew her well. He and his wife, Peg, had been friends with her aunt for years and were friends with the girls. He grinned as he grabbed himself a cup of coffee and sat, his eyes shifting between the two with him. Ashlynn was correct, Frank realized. They are a couple.

"Frank?" Eilis was not letting him get away without saying anything.

"Someone has been in here, Eilis. You were reading that correctly. I can see where things have been moved around from where you leave them. Peg and I have been here enough that we know your place. Declan, I am an investigator but I am also friends with Ashlynn and the girls. We've been friends for years. I don't see any cameras or anything like that. Your place has been searched."

Eilis drew in a deep breath. It was what she had thought. She could always tell when someone had been in her space. The others had laughed at her but Ashlynn had always hugged her and said that was something that would be used of God sometime in the future. Eilis wished that Ashlynn had been incorrect.

"That's what I was feeling then. Why?"

"That we don't know, Eilis. We know that you haven't been mixed up in anything that you shouldn't have. Your job is a safe one from our perspective as law officers. I have no idea what someone would have been looking for."

"Could they have left something else that's not obvious?" Declan was running scenarios through his mind. His work as a software developer had him thinking differently than others.

"That's possible. Eilis, we'll need you to go through your things, seeing if that is indeed correct." Frank's hand went up. "Not today. You need to rest. I'll stop by tomorrow. I understand that Chani is not working. Let her help. We may see something that you don't. We won't intrude if you say no."

"It's okay, Frank. It's about what I expected you to say. I'll do that tomorrow. I'm not working right now." She dropped her head for a moment, knowing that she had to do this. "Is this related to yesterday? All I did was go to Mistletoe, to have some time to myself. I needed that. With what the others went through, I just needed it."

"We know that, Eilis. We don't fault you for that. What we need to do is determine what you may have seen or have that someone else wants"

"Could it be related to Mom and Dad and Uncle Adam?" Her voice was barely a whisper.

"It might be but you haven't received anything of theirs yet, have you?" He watched with compassion as her eyes closed and a tear trickled down her cheek.

———

"No, I haven't." Eilis turned to Declan. "Our parents were murdered. Both of Aunt Ashlynn's brothers and their wives were murdered. That's why we ended up here with Aunt Ash. We thought for years it was just an accident but it wasn't. Brinn received her father's work gloves, Chani our mother's necklace, Darbi her mother's music box. If it goes that way with me, I'll receive something of Dad's."

"That's odd." Declan was troubled by this. "You girls must have been young."

"We were. Brinn was the oldest at 12, then Chani, Darbi and myself. We're about a year apart in age. Aunt Ash was so young when she set aside her life to take us."

"And your aunt has not regretted a moment of that. It's what she wanted to do." Frank rose, setting his mug in the sink and then turning to Eilis. "I'll talk to Chani. I'll send you a message with the time that we can both make it. Don't be afraid to call one of us or the detachment if you need us."

"I won't. Thank you, Frank."

Frank closed the door behind him, troubled that Eilis had faced this. He walked down the stairs, looking for the building manager. He spoke with him at length, the man nodding in agreement. Steps would be taken to try and keep Eilis safe. If it came to it, then he would simply move her somewhere. He knew that Richard and Don would move in with their teams. And Abe and Emma would become involved, Abe with his security team, Emma to research and investigate and

send him the information that only she was able to find
on who it was.

Chapter 7

Frank watched Eilis closely the next day. He could see that she was brittle, as he termed him. She had refuted his comment that she was a victim, denying it with words, but he could see in her eyes that she knew she was. This was Eilis. She kept a lot hidden and always had

Chani stood with her arm around her sister, watching her closely before she looked around the living room. She could feel something off but wasn't quite sure what it was. Ronan was in the kitchen with Ashlynn and Declan. All three had insisted on being there despite Eilis' protest.

"Where do we start, Eilis?" Chani walked away from her sister, heading for a book shelf. "I'll start with this. Where do you want to start?" She turned as Eilis didn't respond, a frown on her face as she watched her sister.

"Eilis?" Frank had approached her closer, watching her and assessing her response. "What is off in here?"

"I'm not sure." Eilis walked through the room, touching items, photos, and the pictures on the wall. She paused in front of one, a beautiful sunset over Lake Erie. "This one, Frank. Something is off about it. I'm just not sure what."

Declan moved in on her, his arms around her.

"How be we take it down and see what it is?" Declan nodded as Ronan and Frank did that. His eyes went back to Eilis, wanting to keep her safe and relieve her anxiety. Only he couldn't do that. Not yet anyway, he thought. He was not letting Eilis walk away from him, not if he could help it.

Frank moved closer as the picture was set down on the dining room table. He slipped on the latex gloves and then began to feel along the frame and then lifted it to study the back of it. He sighed. She knew her things, Frank thought, as he reached for his camera to take the photos that were needed and then pulled the envelope from the back of the picture. Frank hesitated and then made the call to bring in crime scene techs.

"I'm sorry, Eilis. This is now a crime scene. We'll need to ask you to leave." Frank watched with compassion as Eilis struggled with that. "You've been through the rooms this morning, I know. You wouldn't wait for us."

"I did. I went through my paperwork as well. There was nothing there. I just need to have someone search my computer." She looked up as Declan made a move. "Declan?"

"I can do that for you. I work in IT but we should have someone from the force do that."

"We should, I guess. I'm not sure that they could access it as I have to sign in every time that I use it. Just a security feature I decided to use."

"That's fine, Eilis. Leave me your password. And your keys. We'll lock up and I'll come and find you."

Ashlynn drew Eilis with her, handing her the jacket that she needed. Declan was close enough to her to help her on with it. Chani and Ronan followed. Both needed to leave but they were reluctant to.

"Aunt Ash? Who would do this? I don't have any enemies. At least, I don't think that I do. I don't want to face what Darbi and Flynn did."

"No, none of us want that for you. It was hard enough to watch them." Ashlynn stepped back as Declan reached to unlock his father's truck, helping Eilis into it. This was not what she had expected but she should have.

Declan paused, his eyes on Eilis as she stared back at him.

"Ashlynn? Eilis did tell me what happened with her cousins and sister. I don't want that for her, but I do promise to be there for her. I will do my utmost to protect her."

"We know that you will. We just need to do what we can. Unfortunately, it seems as if Eilis is off on an adventure. All we can do is pray for her. God is in control."

Eilis moved through her aunt's home, her thoughts tumbling back through the years. She had been so broken when she had come to live there, just as the others had been. To lose her parents and her aunt and uncle that way? It had changed her life and those of the others. It should not have happened. And they were not closer to knowing why. She had reached out to the investigator in her hometown. He didn't have a lot of new information. It was a long process, he acknowledged to work through that case.

Declan had had to leave at last, not wanting to. He had stood and watched Eilis, finding her watching him in return with a puzzled look on her face. He didn't want to see her hurt, but he couldn't not see anything else that would happen.

Ashlynn paused as she lifted the casserole from the oven before setting it on her countertop. Eilis was in danger, she knew. Darbi, Chani, and Brinn moved around her, helping to get the meal ready. The three men were in her office, trying to make sense of what was going on, without much success. She prayed for them all but especially her youngest niece. Eilis had needed that extra attention and touch over the years. Ashlynn had been careful not to favour one over the others but each one had had a special need that she had tried to reach out and fulfill. Some days she felt a failure.

Eilis watched her aunt before she moved into her hug. She was her rock, the one who she had turned to know for so many years. She was afraid for her, sensing that something was coming quickly towards her and that something was not what they could stop.

"Aunt Ash? What would have been in that envelope? I just don't understand it."

"Until Frank comes and tells us, we won't know. And he will do just that. You know he will. I have no idea who it is that is doing this. Let's eat and then spend time in prayer. You need to be resting and you're not."

"I know, Aunt Ash. Only I can't. I haven't slept well in weeks, and I don't know why. I feel followed all the time. Even in my apartment I can feel that."

"He'll be here shortly. We'll find out what he has to say and then go from there."

Ninety minutes later, Frank dropped his jacket on a chair before he headed for Ashlynn's office. He knew that they would gather there.

"Frank?" Eilis looked up, a question on her face. Her face darkened at the grim look on his face. "I don't like this."

"No, I don't think that you will. Eilis, what have you gone and done?" Frank was frustrated and angry at what they had found.

"Frank? You're scaring me."

"And you need to be." Frank sat, not turning his gaze from Eilis. "It is very disturbing what we found. I won't show you what it was, but I will tell you the gist of what it says." He paused, still very disturbed. "You have been threatened, Eilis, and threatened with death." He heard the gasps in the room but still kept watching the young lady. "We don't know who, but it is a brutal death that they have promised. Again, what have you gotten mixed up in?"

Eilis shrank back against her chair. This is not what she expected. She realized that she should have, given what her family went through.

"What now, Frank?" Chani spoke up, her arm around her sister. "How do we keep her safe?"

—

45

"That I can't tell you. We don't know who is after her. So we can't make plans. All that I can suggest is that she keep alert all the time, be aware of who is around her, and find escape routes and safe places wherever she is."

Chapter 8

A week later, Eilis moved through the downtown area, on her way back to her work. She had tried to return the previous week, but Sally, the owner, had simply sent her home. She needed Eilis well as the Christmas and holiday party seasons were approaching. Eilis was known for her designs, well loved by anyone who received them. Sally was wanting to retire and knew that she would ask Eilis if she wanted to buy the business.

Eilis hung her jacket in the employee break room, looking around. She had worked there since she had graduated from college, loving her work, but feeling that there was more that she could do. Only she didn't know what. She walked towards Sally, peeking at the work board and sighed. It would be a busy day and would only get busier over the next weeks.

Sally looked up, a huge smile on her face. She didn't say anything to Eilis, but Frank had been around, checking out her business and making recommendations to enhance the security. Sally had asked why and Frank had been honest with her. Neither one wanted to see Eilis harmed, but both were realists. They realized that no matter how much they tried, she could still be harmed. Only God would and could protect her.

"What do we have on for today?" Eilis reached for her apron, tying it around her.

"A lot. Thank goodness you're well enough to be in. I don't want you overdoing it." Sally turned, not seeing the look that Eilis shot her.

"Frank squealed." Eilis drew in a deep breath, knowing that he had indeed been around.

"He did." Sally didn't turn around. She didn't need to. She knew the look that would be coming her way.

"I'm sorry, Sally. I'm a danger to be around. Maybe I should just quit." Eilis reached for a vase for the first arrangement that she was tackling.

"That won't solve anything. If you hide, then they go after your family and friends." Sally turned. "What's this I hear about Declan?"

"Declan?" Eilis echoed her word, her thoughts on the man who was taking up her time in the evenings and on the weekend just past. He was becoming a big part of her life.

"Yes, Declan. I know him from church. If he's interested in you, Eilis, don't say no. Pray about it and then see what God wants."

"I know, Sally. I'm just scared. He's already been hurt because of me."

"Do you know that for a fact? Could it have been him that they were after that day? Did you consider that?"

Eilis stared at her before reaching for the lacy greenery that she needed. Her thoughts were troubled. She and Declan had discussed that the day before with Chani and Ronan. Her sister had approached her after

—

church, simply asking them to their farm for a meal. Eilis had been thankful for that. She needed to talk this over with someone.

"We talked about that and just aren't sure. We know that I was being followed that day. But no one can tell us for sure who it was. The truck that hit us was stolen and whoever the person was who was driving it just took off. They left us, not knowing how severely we were injured. That hurts, Sally."

"We know that, Eilis. We are praying for you two. Now, work away on that. We'll soon be open for business and it will likely be a busy day. Take what breaks you need to." Sally hesitated before she spoke again. "Eilis? This may seem a strange question." Sally was working away on her own arrangements and didn't look at the younger woman. "Where do you see yourself in five years?"

"See myself? In five years? I'm not sure. I know that I would like to marry and have children, if that is what God wills. Working here. Why?" Eilis' eyes narrowed as she stared at Sally for a moment.

"I have a proposition for you that I want you to pray over. I would like to retire now that Fred has. I want you to consider taking over the shop, making it your own. We would work out the financing on it without any problems."

Eilis stared at her friend and employer never having expected that. She stammered something before she looked down, tears on her cheeks. She had dreamed of her own shop when she had been in college but not once had she expected it.

"Pray about it. Seek counsel where you need to. I don't want an answer yet. Take your time. I'm in no rush. Not yet anyway." Sally simply grinned at her young friend before she wiped her hands on a towel and headed for the front door of the shop. She unlocked it and then stood, her eyes watching the pedestrians. Sally could feel danger approaching Eilis. Only none of them knew from whom or why.

Turning that night, Eilis' face broke out into happiness. Declan was walking towards her, a takeout bag of food in his hands. He swept her into a hug and then looked down at her. This lady was becoming important to him, and he felt that he was becoming important to her.

"Have a good day, dear one?" Declan turned her towards her apartment building.

"I did. I have news but first let me change while you set out our meal." Eilis almost danced away from him, leaving him grinning at her.

"So, what is the news?" Declan stood to clear away their meal and then sat again, his hands reaching for hers.

"Sally asked if I wanted to buy her shop. She wants to retire."

"She does? Yes, I can see that. Fred's done his work and retired. So, what did you say?"

"I'm praying about it. That's what Sally asked me to do. It's a big decision. I have always dreamed of this. I just never thought it would be a possibility."

"Everything is always a possibility. I will pray with you. Now, where's your Bible? I would like to spend some time in the Word with you."

"We can do that." Eilis bit her lip, not sure how to ask the next question. "We meet as a family on Tuesday nights for Bible study and prayer. Would you join us?"

Declan studied her, seeing how she hoped that he would but also that she had been hesitant to ask him.

"I would be honoured to. Thank you for asking me to be part of your family. I would like to date you, Eilis. I just wasn't sure if you were ready for something like this."

"I am, I think." Eilis hugged him and then almost ran for her Bible, sitting back beside him, a happy glow on her face.

—

Chapter 9

Frank turned from the copy machine the next day, watching as Adam walked towards him. He had purpose in his steps and Frank frowned.

"Frank? Have a moment? I found this today and we need to talk about it." Adam held up a photo.

"What's that?" Frank reached for it, studying. "That's Eilis. And Declan. Where is that?"

"That's a small park in Mistletoe. It was taken the day that they had their accident. Or murder attempt, if that's what you want to call it." He pointed to a section near them. "There's someone standing there, not watching them. He seems to be watching whoever it is that is taking the photo."

"He does." Frank gathered up his papers and paced back to his office. "Who do we know over there that we can talk to?"

"Flynn had some friends there. One is a lieutenant on the county force. They are responsible for the policing in Mistletoe."

Frank nodded, his eyes still on the photo. It disturbed him to no end, he decided.

"Reach out to him. See what he can tell us." Frank looked after Adam as he walked away before he sank into his chair, his head in his hands for a moment. He needed to meet with Eilis and Declan and their families. That was the plan for tonight, he hoped. That

—

was unless he was called to another case to investigate and that was always a possibility.

Adam set his phone back down, a thoughtful look on his face. He had tracked down Simon Gardner, the friend of Flynn, and spoken with him. Simon had been disturbed, to say the least, that the investigation into the accident had not been done. He would investigate it, he indicated, and do that right away. Simon didn't comment but he had reservations about the officer who had responded.

Ashlynn turned from her sink that night, hearing the laughter of her girls as she called them. She tilted her head, hearing Eilis' voice in the middle of them all. She had not heard that for a few weeks she decided. The men's deeper voices mingled with them. They were happy, she decided. She moved to stand where she could watch them. It had been hard, raising them on her own, especially when she had been so young to take it on. Lots of prayer and help from friends had made that possible.

Frank walked towards her, his jacket left in the entryway. He touched her shoulder on his way by to help her finish off the trays that she was preparing.

"You okay, Ashlynn?" Frank's question came with the ease of old friends. Sue had spoken with him, just asking what they could do for her. He wasn't sure, other than to continue on with how they had been.

Ashlynn shrugged, her eyes on Eilis, finding her laughing with the rest. But there was something today that was off about her. She was worried, Ashlynn could see and not wanting to worry them.

"I guess. I just wish this was over. I never expected all four girls to go through this." Ashlynn turned, a soft thank you given to Frank as he approached with one of the trays.

"None of us did. It happens, Ashlynn. We'll get through it. This has changed the girls, made them grow up in a way that no one would have wanted for them. God saw them through it. He'll get us through this." Frank studied his friend and nodded. He sighed then. *Eilis is not the last, is she, Lord? Ashlynn is. And that I fear, hers to be the worst of them all. There are things that are still outstanding from the other three, things that need to be resolved.*

Eilis watched her aunt throughout the evening. She was worried about her. Ashlynn had been quieter than usual. Eilis frowned as she stared at her, seeing something that she just couldn't explain. She turned her attention to Frank, settling back against Declan as his arm came around her, missing the looks that her family was sending them.

"Frank? What can you tell us?" Eilis finally spoke, her eyes moving across the faces of her family.

"Eilis? Can we pray first? We need to do that."

Raising her head, Eilis stared at Frank. Something was off, she decided. And hopefully Frank would let them in on it, she thought.

"Eilis. Declan. We received a photo today from when you two were seated in that park. How many men did you see there?"

The couple exchanged a glance.

"I don't know that I saw anyone. I just felt watched." Eilis stared at Declan, seeing the same puzzlement on his face.

"I don't remember anyone either, other than that one man, Frank." Declan reached for the photo and stared at it. "Who is this man?"

"That we don't know. He was there. Notice that he is not watching you. He is watching whoever it is that took the photo. That means there were at least two men there."

Eilis paled, her freckles showing dark against the witness of her face.

"Two men? And we didn't know! We could have disappeared!"

"Exactly, Eilis. That is exactly what could have happened." Frank looked around, centring his gaze on Flynn. "Adam reached out to a friend of yours, Flynn."

"Simon." It was a statement and not a question. "He'll look into that."

"He will. And from what we understand, Eilis and Declan, this accident was never investigated. Simon could find no record of it. And there should be."

Eilis gasped, not sure that she was hearing Frank correctly.

Declan spoke, his eyes on Eilis.

"No report? You know, they never came to take our statements in the hospital. That I found very odd.

You took them but you were not the investigating force. How does that compromise everything?"

"I don't know, Declan. We'll work with the other force. For now, we don't know who these men were. We need you two to be as careful as you can. Be alert when you are out anywhere. Please? We don't want to go through what the others did." Frank rubbed at his chest, remembering the shooting when Darbi was under attack and how it almost ended his life.

"We can do that, Frank. But it will be hard. We can't be aware of everyone around us." Eilis was growing obstinate and that was not what Frank wanted.

"I mean it, Eilis. And if it comes to it and your lives are in clear danger, we bring in Richard, Don or Abe. That will not be an option."

Declan stared at Frank, having heard of the men. Don, he knew, went to their church and he had spoken with him on numerous occasions.

"I see, Frank. I pray that it never comes to that. But God is in control. He decides what does or doesn't happen."

Frank walked away, stopping to stare back at the house. Eilis would be out there, he knew, living her life. So would Declan. There was no way for them to stop the couple. All they could do was watch out for them.

Chapter 10

Running for the shop, Eilis slammed the door and locked it behind her. It was early morning and she had decided to come in early. It was going to be a very busy day, she knew, and she wanted to get ahead of what was planned. She moved away from the door, her hand on her throat and her eyes huge as she did so. With no lights on in the shop, Eilis would not be seen but she still didn't want to stay near the door.

She could see the dark shape of someone trying the door knob and could hear the creaking of the door as it was shoved at. Drawing in a deep breath as the shape moved away, Eilis dropped down onto one of the stools near her, her purse dropped on the counter. She buried her head in her arms, not seeing the man return. A sharp crack and the slamming of the door against the wall had her on her feet, a scream torn from her. She backed away, her head shaking.

It was to no avail. Her arm was gripped in a hard, tight manner and she was dragged, fighting and screaming from the building. She fought to escape, to no avail. Her feet tripped over one another with the speed with which she was forced to move forward.

Another dark shape appeared in her peripheral vision and she screamed again. The man's curses rang through the air as his other hand clapped itself around her mouth. This made Eilis struggle even more.

The other man who had appeared simply reached for Eilis, tearing her from the man's grasp. His surprise move had startled the man, causing his grasp on Eilis to loosen. He charged at him, not seeing the other men moving in. Eilis was whisked away, shaking with fear, tears on her cheeks. Her abductor lay on the ground, bound and gagged. They could hear the sirens ringing through the air.

Frank stood for a moment, staring down at the man. He recognized him as muscle for hire, a man who had moved into town in the last month or so. He was wanted in many districts. This would be one of many changes that he would face.

"Frank?" The patrol officer approached. "The door to the florist shop is open. Was one of them there early?"

"I suspect Eilis was. She told me that they were really busy and that she had planned on coming in earlier each day this week to try and get ahead. No sign of her?"

The patrol officer shook his head.

"Her purse is there. A stool is upturned. The door was broken in. I'm not sure if there is any other disturbance. The others are searching. I have a call in to Sally to get her down here for now."

Sally waited for Frank to approach her, her arms wrapped around herself. This was not what she had expected. Her day off had been planned for today. Thankfully, she had no real plans and could work. But that did not explain what had happened to Eilis.

"Frank? Is it Eilis?"

"It is, Sally. I'm sorry, she is missing. It looks as if she was in the shop and it was broken into too.

We'll need you to walk through with us, letting us know if anything is missing or disturbed." Frank watched with compassion as Sally struggled to regain control of her emotions.

"What is it with these young ladies?" Sally was grumbling and they both knew it. "Can't they live life in a more reasonable and sane manner?"

"I wish they could. I don't relish having to tell Ashlynn about this."

"No, you won't." Sally paused at the door. "This was locked last night and the alarm set. Did Eilis have a chance to turn the system off?"

"We don't think so, but it didn't go off. Someone from the street called it in." Frank waited for Sally to step inside and process what she found.

"She was here. That's her purse. But where is she?" Sally followed the officer as he moved through the building. "I don't see anything else that is missing or disturbed. Just out here." She sighed. "How long until I can get to work?"

"It will be a while, I'm sorry, Sally. We have to have the crime scene techs come through. And then we'll likely need to speak with you again." Frank escorted her from the building, his eyes watchful. He nodded at a man standing nearby. An undercover officer, Frank knew, who would reach out to him when he could.

"Where is she, Frank?" Sally looked around, disturbed that Eilis had disappeared.

"I don't know, Sally. Listen, hang tight for a bit. We'll get you in as soon as we can." Frank walked away, leaving Sally staring around.

The undercover officer watched Sally move away before he turned back to Frank. He shoved away from the building that he had been leaning against, dropping a note under the window wiper of Frank's car. He knew that Frank would find him and then find him.

Eilis stared at the man who had spirited her away from her abductor, anger sparking from her.

"Where am I? I want to leave." She headed for the door, only to find her way blocked. "What? I can leave. You can't stop me."

The men didn't speak, merely stood in her way. She sighed, turning back to pace the room. She glanced at her watch and sighed once more. This was not how she had planned her day. She should have been an hour or more into the day's work. And who knew when that would happen?

Turning as she heard the door behind her open and closed, Eilis glared at the man who entered. He crossed to a table near a window and dropped a takeout bag on it. He shrugged off his jacket, looking around the room. The room was neat and tidy, well stocked for one in a ramshackle building. He turned then to Eilis, amusement flickering across his face at the look that she was shooting at him.

"Take it easy, Eilis. We're friends. Here. I picked up some coffee for us. I understand that you drink coffee." He leaned against the table, hand extending with a cup. "It's okay. It's not drugged or anything like that."

Eilis finally reached for the cup, still not sure about the men with her. One of the men who had left returned, a quiet word with the one who seemed to be the leader. He nodded, his eyes on Eilis.

"Eilis. I am sorry that we had to handle you the way we did. We needed to get you away from that man and as quickly as possible. You would have disappeared and not been found at all. No one would have known where you were. You would not have survived."

Shock on her face, Eilis felt for a chair and sat. She stared at the man, not sure if he had told her the truth.

"It's the truth, Eilis." He spoke as if he had read her mind.

"I see. Can I leave?" She was desperate to leave, to get to her family.

"Soon. I have left word for Frank through someone else. He'll track us down." The man paced the room, his eyes wandering to Eilis every once in a while. This was not what he had expected to have happened today.

"I see. Okay, I guess." Eilis found a chair to sit in, her eyes closing as she began to pray. She had no idea what was coming but she was afraid.

—

Chapter 11

Frank walked slowly through the downtown area later that morning. His steps were slow and showed how tired he was. He was no closer to finding out who had tried to take Eilis that morning. His face didn't show on any of the security cameras in the area. That was deliberate, he knew.

He reached to shove a door open, the building rough and in disrepair. He had been directed here. Frank prayed that Eilis was here. He didn't want to be the one to tell Ashlynn or any of the rest of the family that another one of them had disappeared. Nor did he want to face Declan. He had no idea Eilis and Declan were heading as a couple but he could see them together for life.

Frank paused for a moment, waiting for his eyes to adjust to the dim light. He could see the debris around the floor and carefully picked his way to another door. He studied the footprints that he could see in the dirt and recognized a lady's prints. He prayed that it was Eilis.

Knocking at the door, Frank waited, knowing that the door would open soon. He was correct. One of the men stepped outside, studied Frank, and then shoved the door open, nodding for him to enter. Stepping through the door, Frank blinked in the sudden light coming in through the clean windows. He heard a sound and turned, finding Eilis almost running towards him. He swept her into a hug, assured himself that she was okay, and then tucked her behind him for a moment. A nod to the man and Frank then turned, his hand out for Eilis', to lead her from the room. Frank shook his head as she went to speak, indicating that she needed to wait until they were somewhere else.

Tucking Eilis away in his office, Frank headed for the break room. He desperately needed a coffee and food but knew that only a coffee would do for now. He grabbed a bottle of juice and detoured by Adam's office, just asking him to come with him, telling him that there had been developments that he needed to be aware of.

Eilis looked around as Adam sat beside her, his eyes shifting from her to Frank.

"Frank? You found her?" Adam's quiet question finally broke the silence in the room.

"I did. Someone had rescued her and kept her safe." Frank went no further than that, leaving Adam nodding.

Eilis stared between the two men, a frown on her face.

"Frank? What happened?"

"What happened? You disappeared, were rescued, and then brought here." Frank leaned forward with his arms on his desk. "Talk to me, Eilis. Tell me what happened."

"I don't know who it was. I was too scared to get a good look at him. I think I want to forget that. Someone else got me away and then kept me in that room. Who was it?"

—

"I'm not sure who got you away. The man who kept you safe is on the right side of what you're facing. Now, we need to let Sally know that you are fine and then get you home."

"I need to work."

Frank simply shook his head as Adam rose to stand with his back to the door, not letting her out.

Eilis sighed. *This was really happening,* she thought. *This is not how the day was to go. I had plans that didn't work out. Lord, I'm angry and unhappy. Forgive me and help me to deal with it.*

"We take you home, Eilis. We go through your apartment. Then we talk with your family. This needs to be done. They will have wondered why you had no contact with them over the day. And I have your purse and phone. Sally made sure that I took it." Frank rose, reaching for his jacket. "Let's get you home."

Eilis nodded, suddenly very tired. She wanted nothing better than to crawl into bed. She walked out with Frank and Adam, not seeing the looks shot her way.

"Frank? Where do we go from here?" Eilis stood inside her apartment door, her eyes on him.

"We've talked about this. You know the ropes from what the others went through." Frank walked through her apartment and then came back to hand her the keys.

Declan paused as he shut the door behind him a few hours later. It had taken some time for Eilis to answer. She looked tired, he decided.

"Eilis?" He simply set their meal down and reached to hug her.

Eilis clung to him, shuddering sobs wracking her body for a moment. She had spoken with her family but hadn't told them what had transpired. She would at some point, just not that day.

"Someone tried to kidnap me this morning when I went to work. A man got me away and hid me until Frank came and found me."

Declan drew in a deep breath. He had felt something was wrong that day and had prayed fervently for his lady. He knew that he had been distracted at times by that.

"You're okay?" He felt her nod against his chest. He just held her, Eilis content to be held, feeling safe in his arms.

"What are we to do, Eilis? How do we keep you safe? Any word on why?" Declan finally managed to get her turned around and to the kitchen. He made her sit, retrieved their meal, and returned to sit beside her. He reached for her hands and just began to pray for her.

Eilis looked up at last, studying Declan as he still sat with his head bowed. She was beginning to love him, she thought. Only it was too soon for that, wasn't it?

Declan looked up at that moment, catching her off guard. He simply grinned at her and then reached for their meal. They were sharing their supper meal these days. Tomorrow, they were both off and planned to leave town for the day, this time for a town called

—

Hope. That's what they needed, he decided. They needed hope and lots of it.

Eilis reached for her phone late that night, replaying her voice mail messages and reading her text messages. She had simply sent out a group text to her family that she had had an incident that morning, was safe, and would tell them about it on Sunday. Tomorrow, she was away for the day and yes, she promised to stay safe.

She snuggled down under her covers, her thoughts on her day before she began to pray through it. Frank was right. They had no idea who it was or why. And that was what scared her. She knew from the others how they had felt. It was not a nice feeling at all, she decided. Now, all they had to do was find out who it was. And that would be difficult, she knew.

Declan sat that night, the drapes open in his office, his eyes on the night sky. To have almost lost Elis today? That was not what he had thought that she would say. He didn't have a right to step in and take over. He just wished that he did.

Men watched the apartment building and Declan's home. They were under orders to bring the two to their boss. Only, that never seemed to work out the way that they planned. And that they could not understand. It was as if someone knew their plans and interfered all the time. They would have to do better, they knew. Their boss was growing impatient.

—

Chapter 12

Simon Gardner watched the young couple walking towards him. Frank had been in touch, just letting him know that they were heading towards Hope. Could he help out with keeping them safe that day? He had shrugged, having no plan, and asked his wife if she wanted to meet another couple in Hope the next day. Eavan had just shrugged and agreed.

Eilis looked up with a frown on her face, something that she felt she was doing a lot of lately. Her face cleared as she recognized Simon and Eavan.

"We have friends here, Declan." She stopped short of where Simon stood, a grin on his face. "Who squealed?"

Simon began to laugh, causing Declan to stare at him.

"Frank. He asked if we could meet you two." He introduced himself and Eavan to Declan. "Flynn has told us what has been going on with you two. Off on an adventure?"

Eilis scowled at him even as Eavan laughed.

"We are. And I don't like. Not one bit."

Simon laughed even harder, Declan joining in at last.

"None of us did. You know what we went through. When are they calling in Richard, Don, or Abe?"

"Never, I hope. I don't want to lose my freedom." Eilis moved towards Eavan, linking an arm with her and moving away.

Simon continued to laugh even as the two men walked after their ladies.

"Eilis is doing that on purpose, you do realize that."

"I do. After yesterday, I'm afraid for her. Someone is after her and after me. We have no idea who."

"That's what Flynn said. Blackie's father, a friend of ours, has started an investigation at Eilis' request. And I hear that Emma is weighing in."

Declan recognized the names from what Eilis had told him.

"I pray that they find the people and quickly. I don't want her hurt."

"None of us do. I almost lost my life to a drug poisoning when I opened an envelope. Eavan there? She was abandoned as a newborn. She didn't know her biological family until a couple of years ago."

"That's so sad." Declan paused at a doorway, watching the two ladies standing staring back at them. "I think that they are looking for us."

"And they will be. Set aside what you're going through for the day. Stay alert and careful. If you let them control your lives, then they have won. They have taken your choices from you and your freedom."

Declan nodded, having already come to that conclusion.

"That's what Eilis and I have figured out."

Eilis looked behind her late that afternoon as Declan drove away from Hope, heading for home. She didn't take note of the cars that pulled in around them, friends who would see them safely home.

"That was a fun day, Declan." She turned to him, a happy glow on her face.

Declan agreed. It had been a long time since he had had fun like that but he would rather have spent it just with her. But he couldn't say anything when someone had taken the effort to try and keep them safe.

"It was. Tomorrow is Sunday. Mom said that she and Dad were asked to your aunt's for lunch?"

"She did? Aunt Aunt was going to do that. I just didn't know that she had already. They're okay with that?"

"They are. They know your aunt from church. Has Frank said anything more?" Declan shot her a quick glance.

"No, he hasn't. I don't know if it's because he doesn't know or if he knows and can't say." Eilis watched as Declan parked and came around to help her from the truck. "What do you think?"

"I think it's because he doesn't know." Declan's steps slowed. "There's a package at your door."

"There is? I wasn't expecting anything." She handed Declan her keys and reached for it. "It just has my name on it. That's odd."

Declan watched closely as she opened it, a hand to her mouth as she saw the contents. He wrapped an arm around her and looked down into the box.

"Eilis? What is it?"

"It's Dad's. His cufflinks and tie tac that Mom gave him when they got married. We wondered what happened to them. They were missing when we packed up the house."

"This is strange." He wrapped her into both arms, feeling the sobs shaking her body. This is not how the day was to end.

"Why, Declan? Why? Who is doing this? This can't be happening."

Declan looked around, not sure what to say or do. He simply pulled out a chair and sat, Eilis on his knee, his arms tight around her. He reached at last for his phone, calling for Frank or Adam.

Adam stood in Eilis' kitchen, his eyes on the package. He reached in with a gloved hand, picking up the box. He listened as Frank spoke with Eilis, hearing her words even as he studied the cufflinks and tie tac. Declan stood and watched, not sure where to be. He turned as he heard a tap at the door and then Ashlynn appeared.

"Declan? What's going on? I tried to reach Eilis and received the strangest text back from her."

"She received a strange parcel. Frank and Adam are talking with her right now." Declan walked back towards the kitchen, Ashlynn ahead of him.

Eilis saw her aunt and reached out a hand for her. She needed her family and to have her aunt show up had to be God.

Ashlynn wrapped an arm around her niece, a puzzled frown on her face. When Adam stepped away to take a phone call, Ashlynn spoke at last.

"Eilis? What happened, dear?"

"Dad's cufflinks and tie tac. The ones that we couldn't find when we packed. I can remember you looking for them. I just received them."

"What?" Ashlynn was shocked. "Who is doing this?"

Chapter 13

Chani stared at her aunt before she turned to her cousins. To hear what Eilis had received had been a shock, to say the least. Each of them had received something that had belonged to one of their parents. This had to stop. Only they had no idea who was doing it to them.

"Is this related to what she is going through?" Brinn spoke up. Her hands were busy arranging vegetables on a tray around a dish of dip. "No, it can't. We've each received something. We decided that it had to do with Aunt Ash."

"It may be, Brian, but we have no evidence of that." Ashlynn looked around. "Now, let's eat. I want to spend some time in prayer as well with everyone. I am glad that all the parents are here. Our family has just grown so much over the past year." She studied Chani, seeing the quick look on her face that she hid. Ashlynn would be speaking with her at some point but not today. Today was a time to relax and just have fun with family and friends.

Eilis grew pensive over the day, not responding as much as she usually would. Her sister kept giving her glances before she drew aside.

"Eilis? What's wrong?"

Eilis shrugged, not quite sure what was happening.

"I'm not sure, Chani. How did you do it?"

"God. You all. Ronan. It was difficult but we did it. Our friends helped." Chani bit at her lip for a moment. "I was talking with Darci last night and she asked about you. I told her what had happened and she is very concerned. I would not be surprised to see her and Doug show up one day."

"She did? I really need to speak with her. Only I didn't like to reach out to her." Eilis jumped as she felt an arm around her. Declan had found her.

"Who is Darci?"

"She's a friend but she is also a forensics psychologist. She does profiles for friends who are going through what you are and what we did. She wants to speak with both of us, I would imagine."

"That she does. Doug will come as well." Chani grinned at the face Eilis made. "He will, you know. Just hope that he doesn't bring any of Abe's men."

Eilis began to laugh at that, with Declan joining in as they had explained to just who all had shown up to try and protect the other three.

"Will they do that?" Declan was puzzled.

"They will. And they likely will be in contact with Richard and Don."

Eilis paused as she thought about that and know that Chani was correct. They would bring in those teams and her freedom would be gone. She knew that God was in control, but some days it was hard. It was hard to remember that He would protect them, even it if wasn't what they had planned.

She wandered her home that evening, restless and not knowing why. She knew that she was in danger. Only, no one could tell her why or from whom. That she disliked. Eilis wanted whatever this was over with. Declan was becoming more and more important to her and she didn't want to lose him. And that was exactly what she was afraid of.

Eilis didn't sleep that night. She instead spent it in prayer and in searching the Bible for verses that would help her to cope over the next weeks. It would not end soon, that much she had determined.

Sally watched Eilis closely the next day, finding her quieter than she usually was. Eilis moved through the work, serving the customers that appeared, and working her beauty with the floral arrangements.

"Eilis? Are you okay?" Sally finally approached her. Eilis had become like a daughter to her and she worried about her.

Eilis shrugged, not sure how to answer. She had found a letter taped to her door that morning, a letter that simply said that she was his and she would soon be in his control.

"I'm not sure, Sally. I'm just so confused right now. I just wish that whoever it was would be caught and I could get on with my life."

"I'm sure that you do." Sally patted the stool beside her. "Sit, Eilis." She watched as Eilis sat before she reached for her hands and her head Davidt as she prayed for her young friend and employee.

"Thank you, Sally."

"They're no closer to finding out who it is?"

Eilis shook her head

"Not that I know of. Declan and I have tried to figure it out. Only, it's not what we do."

"Then call in some friends of yours. You have them that are retired officers, are officers on other forces and are private investigators. They are likely working on this already, just waiting for you to contact them."

"They are. They have all reached out to me. Only I don't know where we would meet. My place is so small and I don't want to burden Aunt Ash."

Sally began to laugh and pulled Eilis to her feet, heading for a door in the workroom. It led to the second floor above the shop, set up as an apartment with lots of room.

"Use this. We're ready to sign the papers, I know. And then you can give up your other apartment and move here. It's perfect."

Eilis stared at her in shock. She was ready to buy the shop from Sally but she hadn't wanted to say anything yet.

"You're right, Sally. That's what we do. The paperwork is all ready?"

"It is. Our lawyers are just waiting for us to show up. Sam at the bank has that paperwork ready for you. I'm not asking a lot for the shop, Eilis. I don't need the money." She named a price that took Eilis by surprise.

"Sally? That's too low." She reached to hug Sally, knowing that she had enough saved from her own work as well as what she had received from her parents to buy the shop without any debt.

"Then, let's go. You can start planning on your move in here. And your friends are welcome to come in to your new place."

Hugging her friend, Eilis then moved through the apartment, seeing how much bigger it was than the one where she lived now. She was ready to make that move. It had been a long time coming but that was all right.

Declan turned as he heard running footsteps that night, reaching to catch Eilis close and swing her around in a circle.

"You're happy, dear one."

"I am. Sally has sold me the shop. I don't have to go into any debt. She's not asking a lot for it. There's an apartment that I can move into. And we can set up there to work through this."

"We can?" Declan hugged her close, a kiss dropped on her temple taking her by surprise. "This calls for a celebration. By ourselves or with your family?"

"My family. Oh, this is so great." She was beaming, on the top of the world. And right now, she didn't care about whoever it was that was after her. They were the least of her thoughts that night. Only the next week would change that and in a drastic way.

Chapter 14

Ashlynn stared at her niece and then reached to hug her. She was the one who had seemed to need her aunt the most but to hear that a lifelong dream had been fulfilled? Ashlynn had been the only one who had known for sure what Eilis had wanted desperately, to follow in her mother's footsteps in floral designing. She had a talent for it that not many had seen.

"You're happy?"

"I am, Aunt Ash. And I'll be moving into the apartment. It needs some new paint just to refresh it and make it mine. I gave my notice today to the building manager. He's fine with me moving out soon. He says that he has a waiting list for someone to rent it." Eilis was still walking off the ground, they could all tell.

Chani was happy for her sister. So were her cousins. They were involved in what they really wanted to do. Darbi had taken Richard up on his offer to train her to research for his team. She was loving it, finding a mentor in Gareth's father, Garrett.

Declan watched her closely, loving her vibrancy that night. He had discussed it with the other three men, who all had shrugged. It was what she wanted, they all said. It would be more difficult for her to separate her work from her home life. That would be Declan's job, they said as they grinned at him. They had accepted him into the circle, the four men meeting weekly for Bible study and prayer. Declan appreciated that. He had missed that from when he had been at

—

university and had a group of friends who had done that.

Eilis stood the next day in her new apartment, paint chips in her hand. She had simply walked away from the work for a few minutes, Sally sending her that way, a smile on the older woman's face. Sally had promised to work for a while, just until Eilis was comfortable. They would need to hire someone to replace Eilis but that was something that would be worked on in time.

She turned as she heard footsteps and her sister, cousins, and her aunt appeared.

"This is lovely, Eilis." Chani hugged her, followed by the other three. "You'll be happy here." She didn't continue but she could see the way that Declan was watching her sister. There would be a wedding in the works before long, she thought. She just prayed that Eilis would survive the coming storm that would threaten to engulf and destroy her.

"It is. I have paint here. I think I'll hire it out. That way, I can get it done quickly."

"No need to do that. The guys have all offered. I hear that Tag, Evan and Shea are heading this way on Friday night and staying over to Saturday night to help paint. Ronan mentioned it in passing and they all volunteered."

Eilis glared at her sister as the others laughed.

"Sure, and I'll just bet that he had to tell them what was going on. They just want to come and pick my brains. They want in on the action, as if they didn't have enough themselves."

Friday night found a group gathering in the apartment, walking around and assessing it, getting ready to paint. Eilis was finishing off what she had to for the night and would soon be with them. Frank had appeared as had his wife, Sue. They wanted to help her, that was a given. It was how they treated their friends.

The following Saturday, the man who had tried to abduct Eilis stood near her apartment building. He was bristling with anger, his eyes on the folks milling around and the truck that stood there, being loaded with her belongings. She was moving and he had had no warning about that. He didn't see the patrol officer who had appeared near him, his eyes on him. The officer approached him, a hand out to stop him from moving away. The man sighed as he was turned and walked away, his hands cuffed behind him.

Eilis watched as it happened, praying that that was the end of it but knowing that it not likely was. She sighed to herself before turning to answer a question.

Late that night, Eilis wandered her new apartment. She was apprehensive, to say the least. It was a new neighbourhood to live where she didn't know her neighbours. She was having second thoughts about it.

Another man now stood in the alleyway behind her shop, his eyes on the lights in the apartment windows. The windows were blocked by the drapes but he knew that she was there and that she was on her own. One day, he would find her and take her away. Only, it would be difficult. She never seemed to be on her own. He didn't understand why his employer wanted her but that wasn't his job to know that.

The light from his cigarette sparked in the night. He didn't know that he was being watched in return, the eyes of the people on the street carefully noting him and then moving to the building. They would keep this lady safe, as safe as they could. That fact they had determined among themselves to do.

The watcher didn't know that he was being watched. An undercover officer had stopped in a doorway, his eyes on the watcher before raising to the subdued lighting from Eilis' apartment. He shook his head. She just had to do that, didn't she? She just had to move to a new apartment, even though it was hers, when she was in danger. He followed the watcher as he walked away, knowing that he had found one of the men. But there were more out there. That put both Eilis and Declan still in danger.

Declan stretched out his legs in front of him, slumping in his easy chair. He was exhausted, he decided, not sleeping well at night. He was too worried about his lady. That worry was just compounded by her move. He didn't have the right to tell her not to, as much as he desired that. He simply had to back her move and do his best to protect her when he was with her.

He reached for his phone, a simple text message sent off to her. He waited, a smile crossing his face as he read her response. *Yes, Eilis, we'll get together tomorrow. I want to bring you flowers, but how do I do that when you are a florist? Guess that's something I get to figure out.*

He grinned to himself. He knew what kind of flowers to get her. He searched the internet, finding the business that he wanted. Declan decided that he would stop in there the next day, just to place an order. He dozed off, not hearing the soft sounds of someone moving around his home that night. He wished afterwards that he had.

Chapter 15

Eilis wandered her shop the next morning, eying what she would like to change. That would come with time, she knew. She turned as she heard the back door, a frown on her face. No one should be here this early. More importantly, she was certain that she had locked it. Eilis crept towards the doorway from the shop, her eyes straining to see in the dim light.

A dark form moved towards her. She gasped in fear and then searched for somewhere to hide. Only there wasn't a place. She ran for the front door, desperately trying to work the locks, her breath coming in gasps. She felt the hot breath from the man on her face before he simply wrapped his arms around her and then carried her back through the shop. Eilis fought him, struggling to free her arms and kicking at his legs. She tried to strike back with her head but was unable to make contact.

Tears trickled down her face as she wept with her fear. This was not her, she knew. She didn't cry. Ever. But this had her weeping in fear and terror. She was carried to a nearby delivery van and dumped inside, the man following her. His hand reached for her arm. The tight grasp had him stopping her from escaping.

Eilis finally stopped struggling, realizing that it was useless. The vehicle had not moved from where it had been parked. She frowned at that. She had expected it to take off right away. She tried to raise to a sitting position only to have herself pushed back to the floor. A hand on her shoulder kept her there.

She began to pray. This was not how she expected her Sunday to be. Not at all. She had only gone down to the shop to walk through it. The joy and thrill of being a new business owner had drawn her there. Only it seemed to have been the wrong move. *God, are You there? Do You care? I know that You do. I could sure use a rescue about now. Only no one knows that I am missing, now do they? How do I do this? How do I get away?*

The van moved away slowly at last, its path twisting and turning. The man seated on the floor eyed Eilis, suspicious that she had stopped fighting him. That was not expected, he thought. She should be fighting him to get away. They always did. This was not the first time that he had done this and not likely would be the last.

He studied her closely as the early light shone brighter. She had tears on her face but seemed calm. That was very unusual, he thought. Not what his victims usually did. He reached for a cloth, surprising her into a whimper as he tied it around her face.

Eilis twisted her head, trying to see around the blindfold and not able to. This was not going well, she thought. She sighed to herself. This is what had happened to the others. She had prayed that she wouldn't go through an adventure but if she did, that she didn't get kidnapped. That didn't seem to be happening, keeping safe that is.

Ashlynn searched for Eilis just before the church service, not seeing her. This is strange, she thought. She should be here.

—

Chani approached her aunt, worry on her face.

"Have you seen Eilis?"

"No, I haven't. Not yet. She must be running late." Ashlynn found her seat, Chani and Ronan sitting with her.

"That's not like her. I mean, if she's late, then she calls." Chani looked around. "I don't see Declan, either."

"He had to be away this morning, Chani. He said that last night. He was asked to speak at another chapel this morning. Maybe Eilis went with him."

"She still would have let us know."

Ashlynn headed for Eilis' place as soon as she could, pausing as she saw the emergency vehicles around the street. She frowned before she parked, locked her car, and made her way to the police tape waving in the light breeze. She sighed. This was at Eilis' place, she decided, seeing the activity around the shop.

Darbi reached to hug her aunt. She and Flynn had appeared, having the same thought. Brinn and Gareth had headed for Declan's. Chani and Ronan had decided to swing by their aunt's, to see if she had appeared there.

"Aunt Ash?" Darbi's voice was hushed. "What's going on?"

"I don't know, dear. I just got here." Ashlynn's hand lifted as Frank nodded to her. "Frank's here. We'll see what he has to say when he can."

Frank moved back into the shop, his eyes worried. Eilis was not here. There was a slight disturbance that they could see. The security system had been turned off. But the back door was unlocked and swinging open when a patrol officer had stopped by earlier on his usual rounds. Eilis had not been there. He had walked through the shop and then headed up the interior stairs to her apartment, not finding her there either. She had simply disappeared, just as the others had.

Frank turned once more as he heard footsteps heading his way. This was not what he needed.

"Chief?"

The police chief paused for a moment, his keen eyes resting on Frank.

"Frank? What's this I hear?"

"Eilis seems to have disappeared, just as her cousins and sister did. We prayed that this wouldn't happen."

"But it has. Have you spoken with her family yet?"

Frank shook his head even as he rubbed at his cheek.

"I haven't. But Ashlynn and Darbi are at the barricade. I'll head out to see what they have to say." He turned to stare around the shop. "She had just purchased this from Sally. We moved her into the apartment yesterday."

"And this happens. Someone is watching her too closely. Keep me updated. Ashlynn is a favourite of my wife's."

Frank watched him walk away, knowing that what he said was true. Ashlynn was a favourite of many people. This hurt to have something happen to one of her family members once more.

—

Chapter 16

Frank walked slowly towards Ashlynn and Darbi, his eyes on her. He could tell that she was watching him closely, waiting for any news that he could give her. He sighed to himself. This was not how he had planned his day. he was to be off that day but the on call detective had called in sick. Frank had agreed to work, not expecting to have this situation pop up. His keen eyes studied the area around him, finding what appeared to be a homeless person watching him. He gave a slight nod. He would find him later.

Ashlynn wrapped an arm around Darbi. The other two were still searching, determined to find Eilis if at all possible. She could feel the subdued sobs that Darbi was trying hard to control.

"Frank? She's not here?" Ashlynn didn't wait for him to speak.

"No, I'm sorry, Ashlynn, Darbi, Flynn. She's not. The shop door was open when patrol came by. We've looked the shop and her apartment over. There is no sign of her there."

"That's what we thought." Ashlynn slumped for a moment, not sure what to say or even think. She shivered in sudden cold and fear. The day was warm for late November but she was still cold. Ashlynn was also very worried. "Where is she?"

"We don't know, Ashlynn. We're looking for her but we don't have a lot of information to go on.

—

Did she have any enemies, any problems, that she just told you?"

"No." Darbi was adamant on that. She studied the tall brick buildings that lined the street. "Could she be in another of the buildings here?"

"That's possible. We are preparing to search for them. For now, I would suggest you head for home, Ashlynn. We'll be by later today. If she shows up, call me." Frank walked away, his hand out for the papers being handed to him. He sighed. He was finished with this crime scene and was needed at another. It was going to be a long day.

Ashlynn stood for a few moments, not sure what to do before she turned, wrapping Darbi in her arms.

"We'll head for my place, Darbi, Flynn. She'll find us there. The other girls will come there as well. We'll plan a search, just as we have done before."

Flynn nodded, a thought crossing his mind.

"Darbi, can you go with your aunt? I want to see if I can find Declan."

Declan stood behind them, a frown on his face.

"Ashlynn? What's going on?"

Ashlynn jumped in surprise as she heard his voice.

"Declan? You're here? Was Eilis with you?"

"No, she wasn't. I haven't seen her today. All I had was a text message last night. Isn't she with you?"

"No." Flynn pointed towards their vehicles and they walked that way. "Frank said that she's not in either her shop or apartment. And she never appeared for church. That's what we're doing here. Brinn and Chani are searching for her."

Declan stopped short, the worry that he had been bearing for his lady confirmed. She had disappeared. That was not what he had been praying for.

"No sign of her?" Declan's shoulders slumped. "I was praying that nothing had happened to her. They didn't say anything else?"

Ashlynn shook her head even as she moved in to hug him.

"Come with us, Declan. We're heading for my place. We'll find something to eat. We need to do that whether we feel like it or not. Then, we pray and plan."

Declan nodded, turning to face the buildings, his heart breaking for his lady. *Where is she, Lord? Is she hurt? Is she still alive? Protect her, please, dear Lord.*

Declan paced the sidewalk in front of Ashlynn's home, not ready to go in but not ready to be on his own. This was not how he planned his day. He had planned to find Eilis, take her out for a meal and then a walk if she was up to it.

Flynn, Ronan, and Gareth watched him, knowing to a certain extent how he was feeling. They had all experienced it with their ladies. They finally walked towards him, standing in his way, causing him to stop.

"Guys? What?" Declan stared at them in turn.

"We understand to a certain extent what you are feeling." Flynn spoke for the trio. "We need to think this through. And I'm not sure that we have enough information to even figure it out."

"We don't." Declan rubbed at his face. "Where would she have gone?"

"On her own?" At Declan's node, Ronan sighed. "I don't know that she disappeared on her own. The door was broken in, Frank told Ashlynn. That means someone took her."

"They did." Declan paced away, coming to a stop, his hands jammed into his pockets. His head tilted back as he stared up at the brilliant blue of the sky. There were very clouds to hide the sky. He was at a loss and knew it. Declan turned, watching the other three watching him. He could see the four ladies behind them.

He strode forward, determination in his very demeanour.

"Okay. Eilis is missing. We don't know where she is or who took her. Let's start making plans."

Ashlynn was nodding.

"Come in, all of you. We need to start making plans. Sue is on her way, at Frank's request. Gareth, Flynn, and Ronan? Your families are heading this way. I spoke with Tag. He's heading this way with Ayron. He said Shea and Breckon were with them."

Darbi watched as the group had gathered in the living room of her aunt's home. They were deep in prayer. Darbi had stepped away, emotions overcoming her for a moment. Eilis was the youngest of them, the one that they had all watched out for. She had been independent, determined to stand on her own two feet, protesting at their care.

Chapter 17

Three days had passed. Ashlynn had walked into her niece's shop on the Monday, meeting Sally there. They had spoken before Ashlynn had walked out and to her own work. Her employer was worried about Eilis, knowing how much care that Ashlynn had given the girls over the years. All of her workmates were looking for her niece. Only no one could find her.

Declan had stood for ages outside of her apartment, his eyes on the windows, waiting for light to appear. Only that didn't happen. He would finally walk away, his head bowed in defeat and sorrow. Declan didn't see the men who followed him, watching out for him. The people on the street were looking for his lady but they couldn't find her either. That puzzled them. They should be able to, given the word was out.

Turning from his computer on Friday, Declan yawned and then rose and stretched. He had managed to keep his mind on his work as difficult as that had been. He now faced the weekend, a weekend without his lady. He had finally acknowledged to himself that she was his lady, the one who he wanted to spend his life with. The door been ringing had him frowning. He wasn't expecting anyone, he decided, and moved quietly to look out of the door.

Declan swung the door open, motioning the group of men in. He studied them all, not knowing some of them.

Flynn grinned at him, holding up a bag of food.

"We brought food and reinforcements. We're here to pray with you and then make plans. Our ladies are with Ashlynn, doing the same."

Declan shrugged, not sure what to say or think.

"You know where the kitchen is. Introduce me, please."

Ronan nodded even as Gareth and Flynn headed for the kitchen.

"You've met Tag and Shea. This is Evan, another friend and retired officer. Brownie here is another friend. The others are from a security team who we are friends with. This is Ian and Nathaniel. Abe is a good friend of ours and sent them to help. Abe's wife, Emma, has a business where she finds people, to put it simply. She is looking for your lady."

"She is? I can't afford that!" Declan felt hope in his heart but also dismay.

Ian and Nathaniel shook their heads.

"You're a friend, Declan." Ian stood beside him, a hand on his shoulder. "She never charges friends. She will find what she can, send it to you and whoever else you agree to have it go to, and also to Ashlynn and the ladies. Frank will receive copies as he is the investigator. Another friend is working on a profile and will forward it. Darci is quite concerned as well."

"Okay, then. I guess I have to say thanks." Declan stood for a moment, a blank look on his face. "What can I do?"

"For now?" Nathaniel moved past him. "We eat. Then we pray. Then we plot and plan, as Ian would say." He grinned at his team mate as Ian laughed at him. "And when we find her, and we will, Ian will offer to fly you away to somewhere no one will ever find you."

"You would do that?" Declan suddenly grinned, feeling relief for once. "We may take you up on that." He walked into the kitchen, finding the men had made themselves at home.

"I like your kitchen." Ian looked around. He was known for liking to cook and appreciated a large, well laid out kitchen.

"It was like this when I bought the house. I just updated the counter top and colours. And of course the appliances. I prefer white to stainless steel." He reached for the coffee pot, filling it and setting it to brew. "Anyone want tea?"

"Coffee works."

The meal was spent in Declan learning about the men and then just listening to the good natured teasing that was going on. He had been astounded to find out that all the men and their ladies had faced danger.

"Okay. Now what?" Brownie looked around, before he was on his feet, helping to clear away the remnants of the meal even as Ian was on his feet refilling their mugs of coffee.

"We pray. Nathaniel, will you start us off?" Flynn spoke quietly, his thoughts on his wife and her sister and cousins. This was weighing heavily on them all.

—

Declan raised his head as they finished their time of prayer. He was grateful for their prayers, for their caring and concern, and for them just being there. He looked around at them, realizing that most of them had been or still were in law enforcement.

"Okay, fellows. What now? What do we do? How do we find Eilis?" Declan was sober, not sure how to continue or even if he could. He stared past them, staring at the large framed photo of a local mill that Eilis had insisted that he needed. He had laughed at her, agreed, and then purchased it.

"Where do we start? When her shop and home were searched, did they find anything that they could tell you about?" Brownie reached into his pocket for his pad of paper and pen.

Declan shook his head.

"Not really. The back door was broken in, the one to the shop. Frank thinks that Eilis had come down the interior stairs to the shop. There wasn't much in evidence, he did say. It would have likely been early."

Gareth frowned as his phone chimed and pulled it out. It was his father, sending off a text.

"Fellows? Dad has reached out to the street. He has word that no one saw anything, not that anyone is willing to say. That is odd. There is always traffic in that area."

"There is. Now, we go to the streets ourselves." Nathaniel rose and paced, coming to a halt where he could watch Declan. He was worried about him. He took the time to send off a text to his team and Emma.

—

Gareth studied the next message from his father.

"Dad's heading that way. He has a contact that he wants to speak with. He'll get back to me with what is said."

Ronan studied Gareth before he nodded. Garrett had contacts all over, given his work as an investigator. If he could find anything, he would.

Hours later, Declan closed and locked the door after the men as they left. He wasn't sure if they had accomplished much but he had needed that, he knew. He needed to know that he was not alone, that others understood what he was going through. His finger traced the photo of a lamp that Eilis had given him, telling him the story of the lamp ornaments that the five ladies had. Declan gave a sad smile, praying that she would be the light that she needed to be for God just where she was. He only wished that he was with her. God seemed to have other plans that he needed to follow. Ian had pulled him aside just before he left, praying with him once more. He had commented that a friend and team mate had a saying, that God had plans and purposes that he wouldn't know about yet. All he could do was trust God and follow as He led.

Chapter 18

Garrett slid into a booth at Jeff's diner, nodding to the waitress as she held up the coffee pot. She headed his way, two mugs in her hands. She knew that he would be meeting someone. He had asked her one day how she did that, know when to bring another mug. She had shrugged, smiled, and said God told her. And that she had to do what God said, didn't she?

He waited, absentmindedly stirring his coffee. He watched the traffic through the window, not looking around as he heard footsteps approaching him and then someone sliding in the booth across from him.

"Thanks, Garrett. This hits the spot. It's chilly out there today." Pat, an undercover operative that Garrett knew, had approached him early that morning, just asking to meet.

"Not a problem, Pat. Never a problem." Garrett studied him, seeing the stress of his work in his face and eyes. "You need to come home, Pat." His voice was kept purposely low, even though Jeff had managed to keep the area around them free of patrons.

"I know. I will once I've found Eilis." Pat sipped at his coffee, his eyes on Garrett. "How is Ashlynn?"

Garrett shrugged.

"She's hurting. This is the fourth one of her girls to go through something. And she needs to find her."

"I know." Pat sighed. He had news. Only he didn't know how Garrett would take it. "I have news, Garrett."

"You do? I wondered if you had when you contacted me." Garrett sipped at his own coffee, just waiting for Pat to speak.

"She's not in town. They moved her away from here. About four hours."

Garrett nodded.

"We thought that. Is she well?"

"She was. The one who approached us indicated that." Pat didn't say anything more. He couldn't. If he did, he would compromise an investigation that was underway. And he just would not do that.

"Okay. So, what is the plan?"

"For now, she's safe. She's not harmed. Not happy from what I hear but she is where she is. I have someone watching her."

"That's good. But we need to plan to get her home."

"We're working on that, Garrett. You can't be involved. They are watching you too closely. Her whole family is being watched."

Garrett sighed, having come to that conclusion.

"We gathered that. Now what? What do I tell them?"

"Tell them? For now, don't say anything. Not for two days. Give me that much time. I need to get back in touch with my contact. That person was working on something to get her away. Only, we're not sure that will work."

Garrett nodded, sighing as Pat rose and shuffled away, the very epitome of someone down and out of luck. He dropped money on the table and then sat for a moment, deep in thought. It would be hard not to tell the others but he knew that Pat had asked that for a reason. He had to grant him that, he knew. He just hoped that the others would understand.

Declan watched as Garrett walked away from the diner before he turned to watch Pat. He knew Pat, had shared coffee with him many times. Did he know where Eilis was or was their meeting about something else? He continued his walk, heading for a nearby store, intent of making a purchase. He just hoped that some day he would have a chance to give Eilis that very purchase.

Pat watched Declan in turn. He didn't think that Garrett had seen him but he wasn't sure on that. He followed Declan, sighing to himself as he saw the store that the younger man entered. A man in love, he thought. And that made it dangerous for him.

Ashlynn paced her home late that night. There had been no word yet on Eilis. Her despair was growing as was her worry. She tried to keep her spirits up to encourage the other three girls but it was hard. It was taking a toll on her and it showed. The dark circles were growing under her eyes from her lack of sleep. Her employer had taken a look at her the day before and simply told her to go home and stay there. He wanted her to work on finding her niece. And he would pay her for sick time. That was just the kind of person that he was. They had shared many a discussion about the Bible and what God wanted for them both.

The girls had each turned to one another and then to their husbands. The men had tried to comfort them as best they could. Only it wasn't working out all that well.

Ashlynn walked towards Sally the next morning, finding the older woman waiting for her. They entered the shop, hoping that Eilis would have appeared. Only their hopes were dashed. She was not there. And there was no sign that she had been.

"Where is she, Sally?" Ashlynn paced the workroom before she reached to help Sally. There was more than enough work for both Eilis and Sally and Sally was trying to cope on her own.

"I wish that I knew, Ashlynn. I would go and find her." Sally watched Ashlynn. "Ashlynn? Aren't you supposed to be at work?"

"My boss told me to take some sick time. I never do." Ashlynn looked around, knowing that she could have worked and should have, but she had to agree with her boss. "What can I do to help?"

"You want to help?" Sally nodded. "Okay, this is what we do. These are the vases that we need. The foam? I'll show you how to cut it for the arrangements that I have to make. Then, we'll work together on the flowers."

Ashlynn nodded, knowing that Sally really did need help. God seemed to think that she was the person who was needed. But she had no florist training. She just prayed that she didn't mess up too badly.

Chapter 19

Pat watched as Declan moved around his yard, his eyes thoughtful. He needed to approach him but was uncertain as to how. Declan was being watched. He had seen the evidence of that. At the moment, the watcher was gone. It was the perfect opportunity for Pat to approach Declan.

Hearing footsteps on the sidewalk behind him, Declan turned, frowning at the man who had appeared. He looked familiar, Declan thought, but then he shrugged off the feeling.

"Can I help you?" Declan paused in his forward walk, not wishing to get too close. He had felt the man outside his house that day. He had emerged to walk around his house to see if he could find any evidence. Only there had been none.

"You can, Declan." Pat stopped short of where Declan was standing, a slight smile on his face. He knew that Declan was afraid and uncertain and trying his best to cover it. "You don't know me, that I understand. I have been looking for your lady."

"Eilis?" Hope rose in Declan and he stepped closer to Pat, suddenly certain that this man meant him no harm. "Eilis? Do you know where she is?"

"I do, Declan. I do. She's not in town. In fact, she's a few hours away from here."

"Hours?" Declan was shocked. "Can we go to her?"

"That's why I am here. I'm to take you to her. You need to grab what you need and then come with me. Hurry. We don't have much time until the man is back."

Declan stared at him for a moment before he turned, walking back rapidly to his house. He grabbed what he needed, locked up, and headed back down the steps towards Pat. Pat pointed towards the street, walking rapidly towards a vehicle, Declan following closely. The two men slid into the back seat of the truck, Declan watching the two men in the front seat before he looked back at his house. He had no idea when he would be back there. His only concern was finding Eilis and bringing her back home.

Time seemed to pass slowly for Declan, although in reality it didn't. He listened to the few sentences that the men with him exchanged before he turned to Pat, finding Pat watching him, an intense look on his face.

"Okay, Pat. What's going on? We've left my town. Are we heading for Eilis or was this a ruse to get to me?"

Pat grinned at the look on Declan's face.

"No ruse, Declan. We are heading for Eilis. As I told you, she is a few hours away from here and has been since she was taken. We just managed to confirm her location last night. We had to put plans in place before we could come and find you. You are needed with us. She will not come willingly. If you are there, then she will."

"Just how much danger is she in?" Declan caught the look on the front seat passenger's face and drew in a deep breath. His eyes moved to look out the window at the passing scenery, frowning. He knew this area. In fact, he had spent many a day here as a youth. "I know this area."

"That you do, Declan. That's why we wanted you with us. Well, one reason." Pat nodded in the direction that the car was moving. "We are meeting up with the police in the area. They will move in, contain the house, and find and retrieve Eilis."

"She's okay?" Declan knew that he was repeating himself but just couldn't help it.

"She is. As far as we know, she has not been abused but we can't say for sure what her condition is until we bring her out."

"You must have someone on the inside. That's how you know." Declan grew pensive, his thoughts troubled as he tried hard to stay positive. His thoughts turned to prayer as he petitioned for his lady and her safety.

The car pulled over near an almost deserted, narrow country lane. Pat jumped from the car and ran towards the laneway, disappearing from view. Declan shifted so that he could watch him, his eyes catching the watchfulness of his two companions.

Pat reappeared with an officer, who was dressed in full gear. Declan's breath caught in his throat. He knew that it was serious but this just confirmed it all. He prayed harder for his lady, not sure what they were walking into. His hand reached for the door handle, drawing it back as the passenger shook his head at him.

Pat slid back in beside Declan, trying to hide his worry. They had confirmed that Eilis was there but so were three of her abductors. This made it more difficult for them. He had spoken at length the previous night with the head of the emergency task force for the area police. That man had just confirmed his thoughts.

"Pat?" Declan finally spoke, not sure of what was going on but desperate to know that his lady would be free soon.

"Declan? She's safe so far. The team will be moving in and taking control. They will be the ones to bring her out. We wait here for that. She'll be taken to the hospital, assessed and give her statement. At that point, once that is done, you can see her. And only at that point. We will let her know that you are here." Pat's hand rested on Declan's arm as if to keep him in his seat.

Declan nodded, having come to that conclusion. He watched as the officer disappeared. His head rested against the car window. He watched the laneway, wanting to see his lady but also despairing of that. Declan watched the wind moving the bare branches of the trees and the heavy boughs of the evergreen trees. He watched as clouds moved in, covering the sky and promising weather of some kind. He just wasn't sure if that would be snow or rain.

Pat watched him closely before exchanging glances with his other two companions. They had met the night before, brainstorming on ways to keep the two safe. They had come to the conclusion that that would not be possible.

Minutes clicked by, Declan becoming restless as he waited. His thoughts turned to Ashlynn and the other ladies and his prayers rose for them. He knew that his friends were working on their adventure as they termed it. They were to have met that day. Declan has simply sent a text to the all stating that he had been called out of town for the day.

Activity suddenly showed on the laneway as vehicles shot down it and then onto the road, racing for town. Red and blue emergency lights lit up the day. Declan's vehicle pulled in after one of them, another emergency vehicle behind them.

Declan prayed, not sure what was going on. He petitioned God for his lady's life and health, for the men who had been involved in the rescue, and for a quick resolution to what they were facing. He felt peace descend on him but he was still very worried. Until he saw Eilis and held her in his arms, he would not be satisfied that she was free and back with him.

Chapter 20

Declan slumped into a chair in the waiting room, his eyes glued to the door that he was not allowed past yet. His phone had chimed and he had ignored it. The persistent chiming finally roused him to answer it. He glanced down and sighed. Flynn was looking for him. Where was he? Flynn was at his house, but Declan wasn't there.

Hesitating, Declan shot a glance at Pat, finding him engrossed in a conversation with an officer. The other two men were outside, he knew. His fingers flying over the keyboard, Declan simply said that he was out of town, that he had a line on Eilis, and felt that he had to follow it up. He muted his phone and dropped it back into his pocket. He prayed that would be enough to keep the text messages down. It didn't work. He could feel the constant vibrating of his phone.

Pat moved to sit beside him, his keen eyes watching Declan. Someone had been in touch with Declan, he decided.

"It's okay, Declan. You can let her family know that she's safe. An officer was reaching out to her aunt."

"They were? When can I see her?" Declan shifted on the chair, finding it very uncomfortable.

"Soon, Declan. She's awake and giving her statement. Once that's done, the officer will come for us." Pat stared him down. "I go with you. That's not an option. You can be sure that they are watching us here."

Declan sighed. That was about what he thought Pat would say.

"Pat? What's in this for you? I've seen you around town."

"I know that you have. Eilis has too. She's been kind to me when she has had an opportunity. I am working undercover, as you know, to bring down someone. That someone had determined to harm Eilis and through her, you. We can't let that happen. This is why I've taken this step. I can't go back there now." Pat was troubled, knowing that he had likely blown his cover.

"Stay with me." Declan turned to him. "Stay with me, and we can work on this together. I know that Eilis would want that."

Pat studied him and then nodded. That would work, he decided. Declan didn't have to offer that but he had. He would and could work with that. He knew that Eilis' family didn't know him. He had made sure to avoid them. Eilis had been different. Pat had been assigned to watch her. Only she had been taken when he wasn't able to, when he had sought sleep. That weighed on him.

His eyes closing, Declan dozed. He had not slept well during the whole time that Eilis was away. His body needed that rest. Pat sat silent and watchful. He stood as he saw the head of the ETF squad moving towards him.

"Joe?"

"She's angry, Pat. Be prepared for that. The doc is just finishing his assessment. Then he can go in." Joe looked past him and grinned. "How serious are they?"

"Dating for now. If she's like her sister and cousins, she and Declan will marry. The other three ladies had an adventure as they call it. Eilis was adamant that she would not."

Joe grinned for a moment again.

"That certainly happened. I'll be in touch." He walked away, heading for the outdoors, his eyes assessing Declan as he passed him.

Pat found his seat once more, his eyes on the door to the examination rooms. He would need to rouse Declan soon. He watched as the physician appeared, searched the room, and then headed his way.

"Declan? Wake up, man. The doc is here."

Declan roused, rising to his feet. He wasn't sure what was going on.

The physician eyed Declan before he turned back to the rooms. Declan walked beside him, wondering that the man had not said anything. Pat kept pace with him.

"She's in there." The physician simply pointed. "You're not next of kin, so I can't say anything. She'll have to. But she is fine." He walked away, leaving Declan staring after him.

Pat touched his shoulder, turning him back to the room. Declan hesitated before he shoved the door open and walked towards Eilis. She was lying quietly, her eyes closed. He drew in a breath at the dark circles under her eyes and the slight bruising on her cheek. His touch was gentle on her cheek and she turned her face into his hand.

Declan studied her before he reached to drop a kiss on her forehead. He looked for a chair, finding one and retrieving it to set it beside the bed. He had no idea when she could leave but he prayed that it would be soon. And he also prayed that this would be over for her.

Eilis stirred, wondering where she was. She sensed that she was not alone and grew fearful. Then she felt the hand holding hers. It was familiar, she thought, as hers tightened on it. Her eyes opened and she stared around in fear. A hospital? When did that happen? Her head turned and she stared at the man sitting near her, his head bowed.

"Declan?" Her voice was low and hoarse, rough from not being used.

Declan stirred, his head raising. His face lit up as he saw Eilis was awake and watching him.

"Eilis? Oh, sweetheart! I'm so glad you're awake!" Declan was on his feet, Davidding over her to hug her. She clung to him in return.

"Declan? What is going on? Where are those men?"

"Which men?" Declan was confused and not sure who she was speaking about. He looked around, without seeing anyone other than themselves.

"Those men! The ones who took me from my home! Where are they?"

Declan could hear the fear in her voice. He sighed to himself before he began to pray again, asking God to grant her peace and hope in this area

Eilis shot up to a sitting position, searching the room.

"They're not here?" He could hear the hope in her voice.

"No, they're not. As far as I know, they have been arrested."

"They have? I'm free?" She shoved at the blanket, her feet swinging over the side of the bed. She launched herself at him.

He barely kept his feet, his arms wrapping around her tightly. He felt the sobs shaking her body.

A sound at the door brought his head around. Pat stood there, a shuttered look on his face.

"Pat?"

"We need to leave, Declan. And now." Pat pointed to the hallway, his hand holding the door open.

Declan simply swept Eilis into his arms and stalked from the room, finding himself surrounded by Pat, the two other men, and patrol officers. He shook in fear for a moment before he felt the strength that he needed. He knew only God could provide that at the moment.

Chapter 21

Eilis' head was down on Declan's shoulder and his arm around her. She slept, her lack of sleep and stress drawing on her strength and depleting it. He looked over her head at Pat, finding him watching Eilis as well.

"Pat? Can you tell me anything at all?"

Pat shook his head.

"No, not yet. We need to get her home and back to her family. Frank will talk with you and them about what transpired."

Eilis had roused, frowning at being in a car. She glared at Pat, who simply stared back at her, his face neutral.

"Where did you come from?"

"I was part of the group who found you and helped to free you." Pat's hand went up as her mouth opened. "It's okay to be angry, Eilis. Those emotions are all part of what you will experience over the next while." He nodded at Declan. "Don't shut out your boyfriend or your family. They will help you work through it all. And I know people who you can speak with."

"So do I." Eilis sighed, her hand finding Declan's and clinging to it. "A lady named Darci has been speaking with me about what the others went through. I'll talk with her."

Pat seemed surprised, quickly covering it but not before Declan had caught his look. Declan had heard of Darci and knew that she had indeed spoken with Eilis. She had even reached out to himself but they had not connected as yet. That would change, he decided. His eyes turned to watch the scenery outside of the vehicle, his eyes on the sky as twilight dropped. He was tired, he decided as well, but was afraid to sleep, afraid that Eilis would disappear once more and this time he would be unable to find her.

Eilis stood in her aunt's driveway, not really wanting to be there. She wanted to be home, in her apartment, and just hide. She knew that wasn't possible. Declan stood beside her, his arm around her. He waited for her to make the first move, letting her know from the way he held her that he backed whatever decision she made.

She looked up at him, finding him watching her, a smile on his face just for her. She sighed. This was not the way it was supposed to be, she knew. She finally made a move to walk towards the door, not seeing Pat and the two other men standing near them, backs to them, eyes watching the neighbourhood. Eilis was still not safe. And that meant Declan would not be safe.

Ashlynn turned from her work in the office, frowning as she heard the door open and close but no one walking any further in. She rose and headed for the hallway, stopping to clap her hands over her mouth.

Eilis stood for a moment, her eyes on her aunt, hardly able to see her for the tears blocking her vision. She felt Declan's hand on her back, gently shoving her forward and to her aunt. She almost ran to be clasped tightly in Ashlynn's arms, both women weeping. Declan gave a sad smile and then moved past them, heading for the kitchen, intent on making their tea or coffee. They would need something soon, he knew. He sighed. This was were it became quite difficult. Eilis needed to talk about what happened, but he sensed that she didn't want her aunt to know exactly what had happened. Her sister and cousins were different. They had all lived something like this and would and could understand to a certain degree.

Declan turned as he heard the ladies moving towards him, his arms out to hug Eilis tight. He tilted his head to study her face, seeing the tears on her cheeks, but also a determination to end whatever it was. And that would be a problem, he knew. They had no idea what was going on. He looked up at Ashlynn, seeing the puzzlement on her face.

"Declan? What is going on? Flynn said he couldn't find you today."

"No, he couldn't. I was taken to find Eilis. Frank will talk with us all about that. He will be approached and briefed by the responding officers." Declan hugged Ashlynn, already thinking of her as an aunt.

"He will? I guess that's it for now then." Ashlynn moved to prepare food for the couple, setting sandwiches in front of them.

"It is. I need to go home, Aunt Ash. I just need to." Eilis stared down at her sandwich, not making a move to eat anything.

"Eat, sweetheart. Then we'll take you home."
Declan shoved back from the table, heading for his
jacket and Pat. "Pat?"

Pat turned, nodding as he saw the look on
Declan's face.

"She wants to go home but isn't sure if she
should."

Declan sighed, rubbing at his face. He could
barely make out Pat's face in the darkness.

"She does. She should stay here but she needs to
take back her life. Part of that is going on."

"It is. She'll get there, Declan. At some point,
we'll talk. I spoke with Frank. He wants to meet with
all of you sometime tomorrow."

"It will have to be in the evening." Declan turned
back to the house, finding Eilis waiting for him.
"Ready to go, sweetheart?"

She nodded before she hugged her aunt. She
reached for the hand that Declan was holding out, his
grasp strong and tight. She leaned into him as they
walked down the sidewalk and to the car. She didn't
look back, not wanting to see the look on her aunt's
face.

Ashlynn watched her, a hand to her cheek. Eilis
was growing up and away from her. That much she
knew. And it was only right. She was reaching out to
the man who God had provided for her. That was right
too. Ashlynn drew in a deep breath, wondering what
she had missed by not having that person in her life.

Eilis stood at the base of the stairs, staring up at the landing at the top. She was hesitant to go up them, finding Declan just wrapping her in his arms and praying for her. She took the first step and then continued up them, unlocking the door and feeling for the light switch.

Declan hesitated just inside the door, knowing that Eilis needed to do this, to take back her life. She had to do that on her own. Neither he nor her family could do that for her. God would protect her and guide her in that. He had no doubt about that.

Chapter 22

The next morning found Eilis in the florist shop work room. She was afraid, more afraid than she had ever been. This was where she had been taken from. She feared that happening again. Eilis moved through the shop, coming back to stare at the work sheets. Sally had been busy, she noted, and wondered who had been helping her. Someone had.

Eilis reached for the top work order, sighing. She didn't want to be there. She was too tired to work but knew that she had no choice. She simply reached for what she needed and began to work. Lost in work, Eilis didn't hear the door opening behind her and jumped as she heard a voice.

Sally stood, staring at her, shocked to see her there.

"Eilis? What? You're here?" Sally moved to hug her and then stood back.

"I am. I was rescued yesterday. I can't talk about it but I was kept far from here." Eilis blinked rapidly, trying to control her emotions.

"All I can say is that I'm glad you are here." Sally reached to hang up her jacket and turned back.

"You've been busy."

"We have been. Your aunt came in and helped. Her boss told her to take some time."

"She did? That was nice." Eilis bit at her lip, a new action that Sally noted. "Are there any big orders that we need to work on?"

"Not for today. Later in the week, we have a wedding to do but I've ordered everything that we need."

"Thank you, Sally. I know that you are wanting to retire but thank you for sticking around."

"I would do nothing else. You're like family to us, Eilis. I could do nothing else." She smiled. "And just where is Declan?"

"At work, I would suspect. He lost a day yesterday and has to make that up."

"That he does."

Late that afternoon, Eilis looked up, hearing Declan's voice. He stood in front of her, a grin on his face.

"Ready to lock up for the night?" He reached to hug her, finding her hugging him back.

"Is it that time already?" She looked around, realizing that Sally was locking up and preparing to leave.

"It is. I will see you in the morning, Eilis." Sally was gone, leaving Eilis and Declan staring at one another.

"I guess it's time." Eilis cleared away what she had been working on, putting what needed to be in the cooler. "I'll need to change."

"That's fine. Don't rush." Declan grinned as she ran for the stairs and then was back in no time at all.

"That was quick. Now, let's head for your aunt's." He frowned as she hesitated. "Eilis? Sweetheart?"

"It's okay, Declan." She had looked up in surprise at what she had heard him say. She would need to talk to him about that at some point, she knew.

Declan stood outside the door, hearing the locks click into place and then her footsteps heading back up to the apartment. His hand rested on the closed door, his thoughts on Eilis and what she had gone through, and prayed for her protection. She was too precious to him, he knew, for anything to happen to her. She was the light of his world.

Eilis walked back through her apartment an hour later. She had showered, feeling clean for the first time in days. Her winter nightwear was warm and she had wrapped a heavy fleece robe around herself. Fluffy socks covered her feet. She was afraid and really didn't want to be alone but she didn't want to be around anyone, just in case.

Ashlynn paused in her office, her eyes on her desk. She had returned to work that day, knowing that she had to. She was worried about Eilis, that was a given. Frank had reached out to her, setting up a time for the next day. She had spoken with the other three, who were thankful that Eilis was home, surprised that she was, and worried about her.

Declan reached for his phone, reading through his messages. He had ignored it all day. He sighed.

———

He wanted to be with Eilis, to protect her, but wasn't able to. Not yet, anyway, he thought. Someday, perhaps that would change. Nothing was certain any more. All he knew was that the woman he loved was in danger and he could not protect her.

Thinking through the day, Declan paused as he reached for his mug. He stared at it, not sure why he was having coffee this late in the evening, or rather that early in the morning. He had given up on sleeping, knowing that it would not happen.

Chani paced the house, Ronan sound asleep or so she thought. She was deeply worried about her sister, not knowing what had happened. She wasn't even sure that Eilis would be able to share fully with them. She had reached out to Eilis, only able to leave a text message that she loved her. Ronan stood where he couldn't be seen, his eyes on his wife before he moved forward, stopping her in her tracks and wrapping her into a hug. His prayer was raised for all the ladies.

Darbi tossed and turned before Flynn simply reached to hold her, stilling her movement. They spoke quietly, knowing how they had felt when they went through what they had. They could make no sense of what had happened or how she had been freed.

Brinn had spoken with Garrett after Ashlynn had reached out to them, asking for his advice. He had simply told her to wait for Eilis to speak, knowing how hard that would be for her. Gareth had listened, his arm around her as his father had prayed for them all. That was what would get them through, he knew. He had sighed as Brinn had slumped back against him. They were no further ahead in finding out who it was.

Emma and Abe had shared a look when Gareth had reached out to them, knowing that this was getting dangerous for Eilis. For some reason, Emma had not found out much information about the perpetrators and that was unusual for her. She had reached for her phone, frowning at the text message that she had received before she nodded. Pat had been in touch, giving her names. She would start her search on the morrow, praying that she could and would find the people responsible before either one had to deal with more danger. Only she knew that wasn't reasonable to even expect that, not given what had happened.

Chapter 23

Frank turned from hanging up his jacket the next morning, thinking through what he needed to do that day. He felt swamped with work and for a moment overwhelmed. His thoughts turned to Eilis. He still needed to meet with her and planned on heading that way once he had sorted through the work on his desk. He looked up for a moment, prayers raising for his friends and then for the situations that he would find that day.

Eilis looked around as she heard footsteps approaching her, reaching to dry her hands off. She had just finished the last arrangement for the day. Her staff were in front of the shop. Frank watched her, assessing her closely. He saw the signs of stress that were evident on her face.

"Frank? You need to speak with me?"

"I do, Eilis. Is now a good time?" Frank followed her as she walked towards the stairs and then up to her apartment. He reached for the coffee carafe to start a fresh pot of coffee, hearing Eilis moving away and then returning.

"Frank? You're here? I thought that we were meeting with the family tonight." Eilis was confused.

"We are. I need to go over your statement, even if it was given to another force. Can we do that now?"

Eilis shrugged, thanking him for the mug of coffee before she pointed to the living room area.

"In there, I think. How is Sue?" Eilis was trying her best to avoid any conversation relating to her abduction.

Frank smiled, knowing what she was doing. Victims did that, he knew, but he also knew that EIlis would speak with him before he left. She would grant him that.

"We need to talk, Eilis, and without your family present. You need to tell me what you went through. At the moment, you can't tell them everything and you know that. You need to tell me. It's not an option." Frank sat, his notebook and pen at the ready, his eyes on his young friend.

Eilis sighed, her eyes sliding closed for a moment. She knew that Frank was right. She just wasn't ready to relive that adventure, an adventure that had scared her more than anything ever had in her life.

"I don't know quite where to start, Frank. It all happened so quick." She blinked to clear her eyes, feeling the terror once more.

"At the beginning, Eilis. Just start talking. If I have questions, I'll ask when you finish. You were downstairs?"

"I was. I had gone down earlier that morning. I was looking around, the thrill of owning the shop so new and fresh that I had trouble believing that it was all mine. Sally gave me a really good price on it and we had signed the paperwork the day before. I was just taking it in, trying to think through what I wanted to do. Only my mind was muddled with so much. I heard the door and turned. The man was there. I tried to run but he was too quick for me. He just bundled me out of the door and into the van."

Eilis had been shoved to the floor of the van, a hand holding her there. A blindfold had been shoved across her eyes at some point, blocking anything that she might be able to see. She had shaken with fear before she grew angry. This was not to be happening to her, she thought.

Allowed to sit up at some point, she leaned against the back of a seat, feeling the rocking of the van as it moved at a high rate of speed. Eilis had no idea how long that had been before the van slowed. She waited for the doors to open but they didn't. She frowned, wondering why not. She was sore from sitting on the rough metal floor and cold.

The van started up once more, slower this time. The road was bumpy, Eilis decided, trying to brace herself as best she could. Once more the van halted and this time she heard the motor stop. She decided that they had arrived at their destination, one that she had no intention of staying at. She would flee as soon as she was out of the van.

Only, that didn't happen that way. Eilis was dragged from the van, a hand grasping her arm in a tight hard grip. She was forced to stumble towards a building that she could not see and then inside. She felt the warmth and was grateful for that.

Eilis was pulled to a halt, not allowed to move or remove her blindfold. That frustrated her. Her head twisted as she tried to listen, hearing faint murmurs from the men before she was once more shoved forward, this time catching her hand on a chair before she was shoved down into it. Her blindfold was removed and she blinked to try to clear her vision, to be accustomed to the light again. It was near noon, she decided.

The men moved around her, one standing nearby, his eyes on her. She shuddered at the hard, evil look that they had. Where was she and just what did they want? That she couldn't determine and it didn't appear as if they were ready to tell her.

"Why am I here?" Eilis' voice broke through the silence. "Not telling me? I'm out of here then." She was on her feet, running for the door.

The man near her simply wrapped an arm around her to stop her and dropped her back into the chair. A hand was on her shoulder to keep her there, the hand heavy and not moving.

"What do you want? I have nothing to give you." Eilis was defiant if afraid. She wasn't willing to become a victim.

"Be silent." The leader of the men growled at her, his voice low and menacing. "It's not for you to know as yet. When it is time for you to know, then it will be explained to you." He pointed a stubby finger at her. "So, be quiet. If you're not, then we gag you."

Eilis grew silent, sure that they would do just that. And she wasn't ready to be bound and gagged for as long as she was there. She had no doubt that was what was planned for her.

Allowed at last to rise, Eilis wandered the cabin, not quite sure where she was or why. It didn't make any sense, not at all.

She was given a room near the back of the cabin. She watched as the door was closed behind her. Eilis sighed as she toured it. Nothing that she could use for a weapon. The windows were not able to be opened. She slumped on the bed, feeling the blankets. This was not a cheap place, she decided. Whoever owned it had money. Only, that didn't tell her why she was here.

Chapter 24

The days passed slowly for Eilis. She was not asked anything nor was she told anything. She was allowed her freedom in the cabin, just not allowed outside of it. She was restless, waiting for something to happen. Only, that something never did.

Then it happened. It was mid-day, she thought, her mind not quite sure any more on what day it was. She looked around at the men, sensing that something would happen that day. Eilis had made her way to the kitchen, under the watchful eye of one of the men. She was allowed to cook for herself, the only stipulation was that someone was with her. She sighed. She wanted to be free again but didn't think it would happen.

The sounds of shouts and then the slamming open of the doors frightened her. She dropped to her knees, her arms over her head. She could hear the shouting continuing and choked on the smoke from whatever it was that had exploded. Eilis was never sure afterwards what happened or in what sequence.

A hand on her arm had her raising her head, anger sparking from her eyes. She stared in shock at the man who was crouching beside her, dressed in his uniform and helmet. She pulled back from him before his tight grip on her arm had her on her feet and rushed through the back door.

Men surrounded her and rushed her away from the scene, not letting her relax. She collapsed at some point, not wanting to believe that she was free. Paramedics were there, reaching for her.

Awaking later in the hospital room, Eilis searched for her abductors, not seeing them. Instead a police officer was there, a detective she said, wanting Eilis to talk. Eilis did, not feeling that she had been of much help in what she could say.

She slept, tightening her hand on the hand that held hers. She felt safe now, she thought in her dreams. Awakening once more, she stared around, her eyes stopping on Declan, not quite sure where he had come from. She was just glad that he was there.

Seeing her aunt, Eilis had just clung to her. Her emotions were all over the place and she just couldn't put into words what she wanted to say. Fatigue dogged her footsteps even though she had slept on the way home, a four hour journey she had been told. She had simply stared at Pat, frowning that he was there. He had simply stared back at her, not saying a word.

Eilis came back to the present, to find Frank watching her closely, assessing her. She sighed. She was now a victim of crime, wasn't she? She hated that. She had prayed that whatever it was or whoever it was would stop with Darbi. Only that had not worked out.

"Frank?" Eilis reached for her coffee, sipping at it, not realizing that it had grown cool.

"Eilis? This cabin? Can you remember anything else about it?"

"Not really. It looked as if it had been stripped of any personal, if anything had been there at all. Just the basics. There were books but not my choice. No electronics that I could see. Nothing really for me to do." Eilis' head went back and her eyes closed. She envisioned the room.

"That's okay. I know photos were taken. I'll retrieve copies of them." Frank looked down at his notes. "You don't have a lot to remember, do you?"

Eilis shook her head.

"Not really. I did give descriptions of the men to the detective. Has she forwarded that to you?"

"She has. She has done a thorough search. We are working through the names on that cabin. It is buried deep." Frank watched her closely. "Just how are you doing, Eilis?"

"How am I doing?" Eilis stared at him, her brow wrinkling. "I am not sure how I am to be doing. I'm scared, Frank, worried. Ticked off." She glared at him as his smile widened. "I know. All the victims say that. And I hate being a victim. I can tell you that already."

"I know that you do." Frank tucked away his notepad and pen. "Listen, we're to meet with your family. Are you up for that?"

Eilis shrugged, not sure how she felt.

"Declan said that he would pick me up. Or are you driving me?" She smirked at him.

"Declan called me and said the same. I have to drop back to the office for a bit. But I promise, I will be there. Just to touch base with you all." Frank stood, his eyes on the floor. "I can't tell you how to look after yourself and stay safe. I can give advice but it might not work in any situation that you find yourself. You have to assess the risks of everything that you do and everywhere that you go."

"I know, Frank. I feel like I am such a danger to everyone around me."

"That is possible. I wish I had a better lead on who it is. And that just isn't clear at the moment."

Eilis locked the door after him, trudging back up the stairs. She cleared away their mugs, set the coffee pot for later, and then looked down at her clothes. She needed to change but didn't have the energy for that. Her aunt was expecting her for a meal and she just wasn't ready for that. She loved her family dearly but for once didn't want to be around them.

Eilis trudged towards her bedroom, reaching for comfort clothes, and changing. As she brushed her hair, she heard the doorbell ring. Sighing she reached for the monitor, seeing Declan waiting for her. Shrugging into her jacket, her purse over her shoulder, she trudged back down the steps, to open and then shut and lock the door. Declan took one look at her and simply opened his arms. Eilis gave a small sound, almost running to him, to be held tight to his heart. She heard his whispered prayer for her.

"Okay, sweetheart?" Declan's voice was low. He wasn't watching her. Instead, his eyes were moving around the area. He frowned as he saw Pat before he nodded. Pat was watching out for Declan's lady. That was a given. Declan nodded before he turned Eilis and with an arm around her directed her to his car. He stood after he closed the door, his head raised, sensing that they were being watched and that not just by Pat.

Pat walked by him, shuffling as he did so. He was aware that there were others out there, intent on harming this pair. He would do his utmost to keep that from happening.

"Head off, Declan. Someone will follow you." Pat's lips barely moved as he muttered his words, his steps not pausing at all.

Declan stared down at the window, seeing Eilis watching him, her heart on her face. This was the lady that he had dreamed about, had watched for, and despaired of ever finding. Only she was here and in danger and he had no idea how to keep her safe. Only God could do that. And that was his hourly prayer, that she was kept safe.

Chapter 25

Chani watched her sister closely, not sure of her any more. There was something different about her. She could sense that she was angry but also terrified. Chani could understand those emotions only too well. Ronan simply hugged her and then with a hand to her back sent her towards Eilis.

Eilis looked up as she felt arms coming around her. Chani had found her. She clung to her sister, suppressed sobs shaking both of their bodies. Declan watched, at a loss to know what to do. Ronan had approached to stand beside him, an arm across his shoulders, and simply prayed for his friend.

"It's hard, Declan, when they weep. We can't make it better for them as much as we would like to." Ronan nodded as Flynn and Gareth approached them. "How be we find a corner to pray?"

"That would be good. Thank you." Declan followed as they led the way to the sunroom.

Finding seats, he listened as his friends prayed, feeling as if he were right in front of God's throne. He needed that, he knew, feeling drained and lost and alone. Only he wasn't. Here were three friends who had gone through something similar to what he was. And God had brought them through. His eyes opening, he stared at the lamp ornament on the wall. He frowned. Ashlynn had moved it, he could see.

Ashlynn hesitated before she approached the sisters, simply sweeping them into her arms. Her own tears wet their hair. Her heart was broken for them. They had lost too much too young and then to face what they had? She was at a loss herself in how to pray, how to help them, or even to help herself.

"Aunt Ash? When will Frank be here?" Darbi had approached as had Brinn, simply reaching to hug everyone.

"Soon. I have coffee, tea, and some sweets. Where did the boys go?"

"To the sunroom to pray." Brinn turned that way. "Can we meet in there? I know that's where your lamp is now. We need to be reminded of that, don't we?"

"We do. We are the light in this world, no matter how hard that is." Ashlynn turned to the kitchen, finding the men had appeared and taken the trays already. "Okay. We'll just wait then for Frank." She watched as the younger ladies headed after the men, her heart troubled. Someone was after her Eilis and she just could not help her.

Frank tapped at the door before he entered, his jacket dropped onto a chair and his boots on the tray. He studied Ashlynn, seeing the worry and strain that she was trying to hard to hide.

"Ashlynn? You okay?" Frank spoke from years of friendship.

"I think so. I don't know any more. I want to end this for Eilis. Only I don't know how to do just that." Ashlynn turned to face her friend. "Sue?"

"She said no to coming tonight. She'll call you later. This is official business."

"I know. I was just praying that she would come."

"I asked her to but she said no. Where are they?" Frank searched the area around him for the younger couples.

"In the sunroom. That's where they chose to meet."

"The sunroom?" Frank headed that way, Ashlynn following. "That's an interesting choice."

"It's what they wanted. I couldn't say no."

Ashlynn watched her girls, as she called them, closely. She was worried about them all but particularly Eilis. She was angry that the four had gone through something and that something also seemed to involve her. They had never explained why they were receiving items from their parents. She shuddered for a moment, feeling that her turn was coming and she had no idea why.

Frank in turn was watching Eilis, finding her watching him in return. Declan had tucked her close to him, his arm holding her tight. He shook his head. He had no idea what to say and that was unusual for him. This was a strange case. Eilis and Declan were not receiving what the victims usually do.

"Frank?" Eilis spoke, her eyes on Chani. "What can you tell us?"

"What can I tell you?" Frank eyed her, a slight grin on his face. "What do you want to know?"

"Who did this? Do you know that?"

Frank shook his head.

"Not at the moment. As I said earlier, we're working through that. But it's buried deep. As to why you were kidnapped?"

"Yes, that." Eilis snuggled down closer to Declan, finding his arms tightening around her. "I don't get why. I wasn't asked for anything. I wasn't asked to do anything. Just nothing. I was just held there."

"Yes, you were. And we can't explain that. The men are not talking. But they are wanted not only here but in other towns. They won't be back here."

Eilis drew a breath of relief at that but she knew it wasn't over. She looked at her family, seeing the compassion and worry on their faces.

"Then, what do we do? I am a danger to everyone, aren't I?"

"We don't know that. I don't think that you are. You're the one that they're after. There are people watching out for you around your shop."

Eilis stared at him when he said that, feeling Declan's arms tightening around her. She sighed even as she began once more to pray. Only God could give her the peace that she needed right then and the protection. She prayed to be kept safe and covered with His hand. She also prayed for her family. She did not want one of them hurt.

Chapter 26

Eilis scurried from shop to shop the next morning, leaving flyers with the clerks. She wanted to run a promotion for her shop, Sally agreeing with her. It was early December at this point and Christmas was coming. Just what she hoped to accomplish with the promotion wasn't clear in her mind. But she felt compelled to do that.

Declan had stared at her that morning when she had told him. They had met for breakfast before they both started their work. He sighed. *She's putting herself out there, isn't she,* he thought? *And I can't stop her nor can I be with her.*

"Eilis? Let me take you out for a meal tonight. Dress up and all." He had grinned at her. They had been spending most of their free time together, either with her family or on their own. His parents were hoping to be back in the country for Christmas but he wasn't planning on that. Not at all. Their plans were always changing and he had come to accept that.

Eilis had agreed and then watched him walk away. Pat had shuffled up beside her, just standing there without saying a word. Eilis had become accustomed to his appearing and disappearing. She accepted that he was watching out for her and that he had friends doing the same.

That night, Eilis hesitated as she reached for Declan's hand. She could feel the people around her keeping her safe. But she could also feel the one who was watching her, the one who threatened her.

"You okay, sweetheart?" Declan motioned towards the street. He had made reservations at a little restaurant just down the street.

"I don't know any more." Eilis sighed. "That seems to be all that I can say. I wish this was over."

"So do I." Declan watched as she settled at their table, his hands reaching for hers. This was not how he planned his night but he would and could work with it.

Their meal finished, Declan drew her to her feet, helped her with her coat, and then taking her hand led her to a nearby room where he ordered coffees for them. He sat her down, watching as she loosened her coat. He sighed. This was not easy, he decided.

"Eilis? You are a beautiful, loving, compassionate lady. I am in love with you. Will you be mine for the rest of our lives?" He drew in a deep breath, seeing the tears in her eyes. "I'm sorry. I made you cry."

Eilis shook her head, raising a hand to wipe at her tears.

"No, it's okay. You surprised me. That's all. You're sure?" Eilis desperately wanted that to be true.

"I am. I am very sure. But it is your decision."

Eilis nodded, reaching to hug him.

"Then, I say yes. I love you too, Declan. I just thought it was too soon."

Declan hugged her back, reaching for her hand and slipping on the ruby ring he had purchased.

"No rush, sweetheart. I just want to protect you and can't when we're not together."

"I know, Declan." She snuggled against him, content for the moment, her fears forgotten.

Declan watched her face, seeing the contentment there but also the fear. He had no way of knowing that things were going to get a lot worse for them in the near future. All he could do was pray for his lady and for himself.

They rose at last, her hand tight in his as they made their way back to her home. He kissed her good night, listening as she locked the door behind her. He could hear her footsteps as she climbed the stairs. Declan turned, heading for his car, a nod at Pat as he passed him. Pat had asked that he not stop and speak with him unless it was an absolute emergency. Declan had agreed, a puzzled look on his face at the time.

Declan slumped into his desk chair an hour later. He just wanted to talk with his parents, have them meet his lady once more, now that she was his lady, and he couldn't. He reached for his phone as it chimed, surprised to see his father's name.

"Dad? What's wrong? Are one of you sick?" Declan rubbed at his head, ruffling his hair even more than it was.

"No, we're both fine. Declan, we're heading home tomorrow. We should be there by the next day. We need to do this." His father, David, was not telling his son everything. The board of the company that he worked for had reached out to him and just told him that David and Angela were needed at home. That their son was in difficulty and needed his parents.

"You are? Oh, that's great. I was just sitting here, wishing that I could talk with you." Declan's voice was troubled and he could tell that his father was waiting for him to continue. "Dad? I want you to meet Eilis again. She's such a wonderful lady."

"She is? The lady who your mother wove into your bedtime stories?" David reached to hug Angela, both knowing that Declan was not saying what he really wanted to.

"She is, Dad. She is just so wonderful. I asked her tonight to be my sweetheart for life and she agreed."

"Declan? You're sure?" Angela didn't like to ask but she knew that Declan would take it in the manner that she meant it.

"I am, Mom. More sure than anything. We're going slow right now, given what she's going through."

"And has that resolved any?" David was worried about his son. He had reached out to Frank, just asking in general what was happening. Frank had told him what he could and encouraged them to come home. Declan needed them, they both agreed.

"No, it hasn't, Dad. That scares me more than anything. I just want to gather her up and run away with her. Only, that wouldn't resolve anything. And we would likely end up somewhere that no one knows us and we wouldn't have the support that we need."

"We'll talk, son, when we get home. We would like to stay with you for a couple of days until we get the house open and ready."

"That's not a problem, Dad. Never is. I'll head that way tomorrow and open it up for you."

"Thanks, son. Now let us pray with you before we go." David was as good as his word, his prayer wafting across the airwaves to bring comfort to his son.

Declan ended the call and then reached to send a text message to Eilis, simply stating that he loved her and would see her in the morning. And that his parents were heading home. He could not wait for them to meet her as his beloved lady.

Eilis hesitated as she read his text, a smile crossing her face before she frowned. She wasn't sure if she was really ready to meet his parents as Declan's lady. But she would. Declan would be there with her and that's all that counted.

She sent a text message back and then sent another one off to her family, just asking if they could meet for supper the next night. Just the five of them. Answers flew back at her without hesitation. That was what her family did.

Chapter 27

The four ladies stared at Eilis the next night, not quite sure that they had heard her correctly. In the midst of her danger, she had become engaged? Ashlynn sighed. This is not at all how she had expected Eilis to become engaged. But then the other three had as well.

"You're sure, Eilis?" Ashlynn hugged her niece, standing watching her closely. She just wished her brother and his wife were here to see this, their youngest daughter set to marry the love of her life. God was in control, Ashlynn knew. But she still was highly worried about her niece.

"I am, Aunt Ash. I am." Eilis was glowing, happy in her love, but still worried about Declan. They had spoken as she was getting ready to leave to meet her family.

Declan had pocketed his phone, his head bowing for a moment. He knew that his parents were on the way but where did that leave them? He had reached out to Frank earlier, only able to leave a voice mail. That had frustrated him. He wanted to know that this was over and over now.

Walking towards his parents' home, Declan's steps slowed. He felt uneasy about being there and he had no idea why. It was the home that he had grown up in. He stood on the front sidewalk, staring at it, his thoughts traveling back in time to when he was young. Declan smiled at the memories. He finally walked up the steps and unlocked the door. He didn't need the lights at the moment, he decided, but would turn them on later.

He stopped in the kitchen, setting down the bags of fresh goods that he had purchased, placing the goods away before he folded the reusable bags to take with him. He walked through the house, checking for dust and anything that needed to be done. His parents had hired a cleaning service who had been through that day, their weekly visit he knew.

Declan stood in the room that had been his as a youth. He reached for the light switch, flicking it on and then walking over to drop to the bed. This was an end of his life here, he knew. Even though he had had his own home for years, this had still been his bedroom. Now, God willing, a grandson or granddaughter would use it on sleepovers with their grandparents. He smiled at the thought.

Hearing a slight sound, Declan frowned. There should not be anyone in the house. That had sounded like the back door closing. He quietly edged his way down the stairs, his hand running down the dark oak banister. His head tilted as he listened, not sure that he had even heard anything. His steps took him towards the kitchen where he paused. Declan's head tilted as he listened. He definitely heard something but there should not be anyone here but himself.

He moved slowly forward, pausing every few steps to tilt his head and listen. His hand reached for the door to the mudroom, intent on opening in and then heading into the garage. The sudden movement of the door pulling away from him startled him. He was jerked forward, losing his balance as he did so.

A blow to his back drove him to his knees and one hand. The other hand reached around to his back while his face contorted with pain. He felt the blows that began, driving him to the floor. His vision faded as the blows continued, unaware of the kicks that combined with the blows to drive him deeper into the darkness.

The man stood, pulling off the leather gloves that had protected his hands and stuffing them into a pocket. He looked around before he walked back through the doors to the garage, hitting the button to close the garage door and running out under the lowering door. He stared at the keys in his hand before he ran for Declan's car, into it and driving away before anyone could see him. He had scouted out the area, noting where there were security cameras and where there weren't. That deed had kept him alive and anonymous many times.

The dusk deepened in the house but Declan laid still, not aware of what was around him. The darkness inside him was deep and painful. He just couldn't rouse or move.

Eilis stared at her phone, frowning. Declan was to have called her and hadn't. That was unusual for him. He always called her, even if he was on his way to see her. She paced her apartment, frowning at her phone. Something had to have happened.

Whirling around, Eilis grabbed her jacket and keys and ran down the stairs. The door was locked behind her as she ran for her car, starting it and driving away. She didn't see Pat watching her before he headed for his own vehicle, driving off after her. There was word on the streets that something was to happen to one of them, just what Pat had not been able to confirm.

Eilis pulled to a stop in Declan's driveway, a frown on her face. His car was there but there were no lights on in the house. She was out of her car, running for the door. Pushing at the doorbell, she could hear it ringing but didn't hear Declan coming towards it.

A hand on her shoulder had her jumping and screaming. She spun to stare at Pat, who had jumped himself at her scream.

"Pat? What are you doing here?" She could barely get her words out.

"Looking after you. Where's Declan?" He looked around her at the door.

"I don't know. I had dinner with my family but he was to be meet me for coffee. Only he never showed and never called. That is not him." Eilis spun back to stare at the door before she had her face to the window, her hands bracketed around her face, to stare through the glass, desperate to see Declan coming towards her.

"Do you have a key?" Pat had to ask the question twice before Eilis looked at him.

"No, I don't. I don't know who has a key. Declan never said. Where is he?" Eilis stepped off the porch and headed for his car, missing Pat's hand reaching for her.

Pat sighed, headed after her and stopped her with a hand to her arm.

"Wait, Eilis. Let me look." Pat waited patiently for her to look at him. "I need to do this for you." He pointed to where she had stopped. "Do not move from here."

Eilis finally nodded, her face white, fear in her eyes. Declan was missing, that much she knew. Only who or why was the question that they could not answer.

Pat studied Declan's car, reaching to tug at the door handle and finding the door locked. He Davidt to look through the window, not seeing anything that was odd. He sighed as he straightened up. He walked around the house, not seeing anything that was obviously wrong. As he rounded the garage, Pat studied Eilis who was still standing where he had asked her to, a woebegone look on her face. This is not how her night should end, he thought. She should be with her beau and he was nowhere to be found.

Eilis looked up as she heard Pat's footsteps, hope on her face, hope that died as she saw the grim look on his face and the negative shake of his head.

Chapter 28

Pat walked towards Frank as Frank shut his car door. He had tucked Eilis back into her car, a patrol officer standing nearby. There were others searching the yard and neighbourhood without any success.

"Pat? What's going on? I just got your message."

"Declan's missing. Eilis said he never called and she came here looking for him. His car is here and locked. We're not getting any answer at the door."

"You're not? That's not like him." Frank drew in a breath and then blew it out. This was not what he had wanted to hear. Declan wasn't supposed to go missing. Not like this, he decided. "How's Eilis?"

"Worried. She's not saying much. Did you know that they're engaged?" Pat was frustrated at the turn of events.

"I had heard that. Just in the last couple of days." Frank headed for the garage and then around to the back of the house. "Declan told me where he hid a key. I have no idea why he did that but he did." Frank searched for the hiding place and retrieved the key. "Let's head in and see what is there."

"Does he have a security system?" Pat was on Frank's heels, not wanting to be left behind.

"He does but I have a code to it. We agreed to that." Frank walked through the house, not finding anything out of the ordinary. "This is odd, Pat. He should be here. There is nothing out of place." Frank paused in the kitchen before he headed back to the outdoors, locking the door behind him.

"Where is he then?" Pat spun in a circle, not feeling that he was being watched. And that had been a constant over the time that he had been watching Eilis.

"I have no idea. I sent a patrol vehicle to his parents to take a look around there. I'm not sure if he would be. His car would be there if he was." Frank stopped walking, his eyes on Eilis' car, watching her as she huddled against the wheel. He could see the despair in her demeanour.

"She's hurting, Frank, and not just from this. What her cousins and sister went through are weighing heavily on her."

"It is. And there is that situation with what they've received from their families. That doesn't make sense."

"No, it doesn't. Not at all, if you think that it applies to the ladies. I think it applies to Ashlynn and someone is trying to get to her through her girls." Pat and Frank had talked about this many times, both puzzled by that.

"I think so too. I just worry about Ashlynn. I fear that she will face something much worse than her girls have." Frank rubbed at his face, feeling the cold of the night beginning to set in.

———

Eilis was out of her car, running towards Frank, seeing him as a friend and not the officer that he was. She threw herself at him, feeling him hug her back.

"Frank? Any sign of Declan?" She was hopeful, they could tell, as she stepped back, slightly embarrassed by her actions.

"No, there isn't, Eilis. I'm sorry. I was able to get into his house and look around. Nothing is out of order there. He's not there. He didn't say anything?"

"No. We talked around lunchtime. He knew that I was meeting with my family tonight. We were to talk when I got home. That would have been around eight. He never called and didn't answer any of my messages. Where is he?"

"I don't know, Eilis. We'll be looking for him. Now, we need to get you home." Frank directed her back to her car and watched as she sat behind the wheel, closing the door behind her. He was deeply worried about her.

"I'll follow her, Frank. I'll get her home safe." Pat walked to his car, his phone out to call in his team as he called them. They would be around the shop to watch out for her. He planned to find a way to get one of the ladies inside there. Only he wasn't sure how that would work.

Eilis paced her apartment, not willing to settle. She stopped at the lamp ornament on her wall, her fingers resting against it. She remembered the verses the lamp was based on and sighed. She was sad that night and wanted Declan to walk through the door or call her. That wasn't happening.

She sank onto her couch, a blanket wrapped around her. The light was low in the room, just enough so that she could read. She reached for her Bible, searching for the verses on protection and hope, all that she could find. She needed that. Setting aside the Book, she wept, her sobs loud in the room. She just needed her family and Declan and none of them were there.

Eilis didn't hear the key in the door or the footsteps on the stairs. She jumped as she felt arms around her and leaned against her sister. Somehow, Chani knew that her sister had needed her and had said that to Ronan. Ronan had agreed, simply reaching to hug his wife and stating that he would drive her in and stay with them.

Chani hugged her sister, not quite sure what was going on. She waited for Eilis to compose herself, knowing that it would take time. Ronan had walked through to the kitchen, prepared their tea and set the tray on the coffee table before grabbing his jacket. He had thought he saw movement in the alleyway and wanted to check it out.

Pat watched as Ronan emerged, evidently seeking something. He walked towards him, his footsteps as quiet as he could make them. Ronan spun and then sighed. He knew this man.

"Ronan? Chani's here?"

"She is, Pat. She just had to. She doesn't know why." Ronan was puzzled but confident in his wife's decision.

"I'm glad someone is here." Pat hesitated before he spoke once more. His eyes were in constant motion, seeking for someone who should not be there. So far, that person had not appeared. His friends on the streets were looking for Declan and watching out for Eilis.

"What's going on?" Ronan turned up his jacket collar, trying to keep the cold at bay.

"Declan is missing. He was to have called Eilis tonight and hasn't."

Ronan's hands stilled. This is what they had all fear, that one of the couple would disappear. They had expected it to be Eilis, not Declan.

"So, what do we do? How do we find him? Or can we even do that?"

"We're looking for him, Ronan. And we will find him. Don't even think that we won't."

"I know. But the condition we find him in? That's what's worrying me. Has anyone reached out to his parents?" Ronan knew them from church but not well enough to call them.

"I'm not sure. Frank likely will reach out to them." Pat pointed to the building. "In you go, Ronan. I gather you two are here for the night." He walked away, leaving Ronan staring after him and then staring at the light coming from the building.

Chapter 29

Frank sorted through the papers on his desk and then rose. He headed for the room that held the recent filings for the cases that were being worked on. Searching for the case file that he wanted, he paused before shaking his head. He had had to set Eilis' case to the side for the moment. Declan was actively being searched for but he had another case that required his attention.

Three hours later, Frank rose once more, this time to grab his jacket and head for the outdoors. He had been in the office early, without taking time for a meal, and that he really needed. He headed for Jeff's cafe, waving at Jeff as he passed through to a booth at the back.

Pat raised his head as Frank slid in across from him. He had news, of sorts, he thought, but no sign of Declan. That had not been for lack of searching. The man had just disappeared without a trace.

"Pat? Any news?" Frank stirred at his coffee, his eyes turned towards the outside of the building.

"No. And we have been searching. He has just disappeared. Just like the others did."

"That's about what I thought you would say. We haven't found him either." Frank sipped at his coffee, nodding at the waitress as she approached to take his order.

Pat watched Frank closely, seeing the stress on his face and his fatigue.

"Where do we go then, Frank?" Pat was getting ready to come in from the streets, to take a position with the investigation squad. That would happen soon.

"I don't know, Pat. I am at a loss. Do you have any word on his parents? I tried reaching out to them without any luck."

"No, not a word. They've been overseas for a while now. I would think that they would be home soon."

"So would I."

Talk turned to other matters before Frank rose, his check in his hand, stopping to pay before he walked back towards his car. He headed for Declan's parents' home, sitting and watching it for a few moments before he was out of the car and walked the perimeter of the yard and then the outside of the house. He tried the doors, finding them locked. He was frustrated that he could not find Declan, no matter how he searched.

Late that afternoon, a car stopped in the driveway and a couple emerged. They stood, staring at the home, before the man moved to open the trunk and remove their bags, the lady waiting for him. They walked towards the house, quiet conversation between them.

David waited as Angela unlocked the door and turned on the hallway lights before he set the bags down and stretched. It had been a long flight home but they were glad to be home.

"We need to call Declan, David." Angela moved to turn on the lights in the living room. "We were supposed to go to his place."

"I know. But he's not answering. That I don't understand. He always does." David grabbed their bags, headed up the stairs and dropped them in the bedroom. He paused, a sudden deep fear for his son rising in his heart. He didn't know why but God was impressing on him that Declan was in danger.

David turned as he heard Angela scream and then call for him. He could hear the fear in her voice and ran for the stairs, almost falling down them in his rush. His socked feet slipped on the polished hardwood floor as he ran for the kitchen.

Angela was on her knees, turning Declan to his back. She had walked into the kitchen, hesitating as she reached for the light switch. Something was off or wrong in the room. Only she had no idea just what. That was, until she walked further into the room and saw her son, sprawled in an awkward position on the floor, not moving. She had screamed, called for David, and then scrambled across the room to drop beside him

David was on Declan's other side, reaching for a wrist, his head dropping as he realized that his son was still alive. He had no idea what had happened but Declan needed help and help quickly.

Frank raised his head from his desk as he heard running footsteps coming his way. A patrol officer burst into his office, not a common happening.

"Wayne?" Frank threw down his pen and rose.

<hr>

"Declan. He's at his parents' place. They wanted him there for now."

"At David's? Is he okay?" Frank was on the move, his jacket on and reaching for his keys.

"No, he's not. An ambulance is on the way. I guess he's unconscious."

Frank paused, a frown on his face.

"He must have been there yesterday. And no one knew." Frank turned to Wayne. "Wayne, head for Eilis. Just tell her that we need her at the hospital, that we have found Declan. And then call her aunt."

Frank approached the kitchen in the house, his eyes on Angela and David before he stopped near them. His eyes dropped then to the commotion in front of them. He drew in a deep breath before he moved forward and around the couple. Frank dropped down into a crouch, studying Declan. His breath drew in sharply at the pain on the younger man's face.

"Tom? Talk to me." Frank's voice was kept low.

"He's been beaten and that badly, Frank. About twenty-four hours is my guess." Tom shot Frank a look before he was back to assessing Declan, with the goal of getting him on the way to the hospital as soon as they could.

"A day?" Frank was shocked. "That's why we couldn't find him. We've been looking for him. I walked around here this morning."

"From what I gather, there were no signs that anyone was here. His mom found him." Tom was growing angry. He was a friend of Declan's. He wanted whoever it was that had left his friend in this way. "This is not the homecoming that they deserved. No one should find a family member like this."

"No, they shouldn't. I have an officer riding with you. He stays with Declan." Frank took one last look at Declan before he was on his feet. He moved towards David and Angela, finding Angela staring at her son. David was watching him, a frown on his face. "David? Angela?"

"Frank? You're here? What is going on? I know that Declan was in difficulty. I just never expected this." David's voice shook with his emotions. "Declan must have come in here yesterday. The officer said that there was fresh food in the fridge."

"I'm sure that he was. We've been trying to track him down. I was here this morning but nothing seemed out of order." Frank's hand drew them to one side as the stretcher was wheeled past them. "You've given your statements?"

"We have." Angela was torn, wanting to stay and speak with Frank but also wanting to go with her son.

"I have an officer here that will drive you to the hospital. Just leave your keys and we'll lock up for you. It will be a while before you can come back in here."

Frank followed them to the door, a quiet word with an officer who directed them to his vehicle and then left with them, following the ambulance that held their son. None of them knew just how seriously

Declan was hurt. Frank's prayers followed them before he turned once more to re-enter the house and begin the investigation that he had prayed he never had to.

Chapter 30

Turning from her work counter, Eilis stared at the officer who had come to find her. She had just finished her last task for the day and was cleaning. Her front staff was leaving as the officer entered.

"George? What is it?" Eilis stared at him, waiting for him to speak. When he didn't, she turned back to moving her tools back to where they belonged.

"Eilis? Are you done for the day? Can you leave?" George stood, his hat in his hand, waiting for Eilis to speak.

"I can. The front is locked up. I've done the cash. Why?" She didn't turn back, missing the sadness on his face.

"I need you to come with me. I need to take you to the hospital." He was not ready for the speed with which she spun around, a hand out to help her balance.

"The hospital? Not Aunt Ash! Or one of the girls!" She waited, seeing the answer on his face. "Declan? You've found Declan?"

"We have, Eilis. That's why I'm here. To take you to him. Go, get your jacket and purse. I'll be at the door waiting for you." He watched as Eilis flew for the stairs, up them, stumbling on them as she tried to rush. He was ready for her when she flew back down, a hand out for her keys. "Set your alarm, Eilis, and then I'll lock up."

George parked at the hospital, a hand out to stop Eilis from jumping from the patrol vehicle.

"Wait until I come around. This would be a perfect time to nab you and disappear with you." George was around the car and helping her out, nodding as other officers moved in.

Eilis hesitated for a moment, looking around. She didn't see her family there yet and just needed them. She moved forward at a nudge from George.

David and Angela looked up as they heard the door, frowning for a moment. Angela drew in a deep breath and then was on her feet, walking quickly towards Eilis.

Eilis paused as Angela appeared, frowning at her in turn.

"Eilis? It is Eilis, isn't it?" Angela's arms reached to hug her. "I'm Declan's mother, Angela. We know you from church but I don't know that we have ever spoken. Come sit with David and me. Unless your family is here."

Eilis sniffed, trying to control her tears even as her head shook.

"Not yet. I need to call them." She hugged Angela back, needing that connection with Declan that the older lady provided. She tuned out the noise and commotion around her, not hearing the steps approaching her.

David simply reached to encircle the two ladies with his arms, his eyes on Eilis's face. He nodded.

God, You did good, he thought. She's who Declan needs.

Ashlynn paused for a moment, watching Eilis before she recognized Declan's parents. She moved forward, Chani and Ronan beside her, a hand going out to Eilis' back.

Eilis turned at that, fighting to free herself to get to her aunt. Ashlynn simply held her niece as she wept before she nodded at Angela. David directed the ladies to seats before he stood back, Ronan beside him.

"David?" Ronan's voice roused David from his thoughts.

"Ronan? You're here?" David was surprised, his eyes watching the people in the waiting room.

"I am. Chani's my wife. Her cousins and their husbands are on their way." Ronan hesitated, not sure what to say. "Where did they find Declan?"

"Where? In our kitchen. We had just arrived home. I had gone upstairs and Angela headed for the kitchen. I heard her scream and ran. He's been beaten Ronan. Beaten badly."

Ronan nodded, having come to the conclusion that something had happened to him.

"What can we do for you?"

David shrugged, his eyes on Frank as he walked past them towards the rooms.

"For us? I really don't know. Until we know how Declan is, we won't know." David sighed, his heart heavy for his son and his lady. "Declan called me two days ago, just to let me know that they were engaged. We were getting ready to come home. Someone had reached out to my company and we were being sent home because Declan needed us. We did not expect this. We had just gone back there."

"None of us did. I can tell you that much." Ronan pointed to some chairs. "How be we have a seat near our ladies? It's going to be a while. I know that from experience."

David stared at him for a moment, not quite sure what he had meant.

"Chani and I went through some pretty rough stuff as did Brinn and Gareth and Darbi and Flynn." Ronan was exhausted, his day long and about to get even longer.

"I see. I wasn't aware of that." David's eyes closed for a moment. He was fatigued, the flight home long and the worry great.

"David?" Angela shifted to reach for his hand. "Any word?"

"Not yet. Frank's back there. Maybe soon." His arm was out to hug his wife.

Ronan watched his wife before he moved to sit beside her. Her hand reached for his. His head tilted as he studied Eilis. *She's taking this hard, Lord, just as we knew that she would. Protect her and Declan. Heal him. Find the ones responsible and bring them to justice. You know already who they are. We don't. But dear Lord, let it be soon. I don't know that any of these ladies can go through much more.*

Ashlynn watched her niece, raising her own prayers for her. She didn't have many details, not even where Declan had been found. She had not asked any details, simply nodding as the officer had asked her to come with him, that Declan had been found and that Eilis needed her.

"Aunt Ash? Where is God?" Eilis' voice showed her worry and devastation. Her faith was taking a beating.

"God? Where is He? He's here, Eilis. He has you and Declan covered with His hand. He has His arms around you. He is covering you with His wings, just like a bird does with her babies. God will not forsake you, Eilis, not ever."

"I know, Aunt Ash. It's just hard right now. I can't feel Him or see Him and I need that." She swiped at the tears that were falling, unable or unwilling to stop them.

"He knows that, dear. He sees your worry and fear. He sees your tears. Remember that He saves each one in a bottle."

Eilis had turned to her aunt, watching her face closely. This was not the first time the two ladies had had a discussion of this kind.

"Will he live, Aunt Ash?" Her voice was barely audible.

"We don't know, Eilis. We pray that he will. God will be there each moment. And so will we. And Declan's parents are here too." Ash hugged her niece, her own tears making it difficult to see.

None of them watched as police officers milled around inside and outside, alert for anything and anyone that seemed out of place. They didn't see the woman perched on a chair across the room from them, intent on a book apparently but her eyes were on Eilis. Malice sparked from them. Ronan watched her, a frown on his face. He knew the lady, just couldn't place her but at some point he knew that he would.

Chapter 31

Frank walked through the emergency department, looking for the officer who had been sent with Declan. He found him, his eyes alert and on the young man as he was assessed. He turned as he felt Frank touch his shoulder and motion him away from the room. They stood where they could watch Declan.

"What's the word?" Frank's eyes were on the move, watching everyone in the area.

"I haven't heard yet. He hasn't been awake yet, if that's what you are asking. They're still assessing him. Eilis is here?"

"She is. So are Ashlynn and Chani. Declan's parents are here." Frank sighed. This was not how he had planned his evening. He had had to phone Sue and cancel their dinner plans. She had been understanding but still disappointed.

"They are? Good." The officer moved as he watched the physician turn and head their way.

"Doc?" Frank stopped him on the way by. "What's the word?"

"Frank? You're here? Of course, you are." Doc Wilson pointed back towards Declan. "We're taking him for imaging. Then we need to find his family."

"David and Angela are here. And his fiancée is."

"He's engaged? Do we know her?" Doc Wilson's keen but tired eyes studied Frank.

"We do. It's Eilis Whitman."

"Eilis? Good. She's got a head on her shoulders. Give us about twenty minutes and then we'll get them back here." He paused as he went to walk away. "Find whoever it was that did this, Frank. They left him to die."

Frank drew in a deep breath, hearing what the physician was not saying.

"He's right, you know." The officer nodded after Doc Wilson.

"I know. That's what hurts about this. All he did was go there to make sure his parents had fresh food and that the house was ready for them. This should not have happened." Frank walked away, his phone out, listening to the voice on the other end. He pocketed it, a grimace in place. It was what he thought. No prints. Nothing to show how the man got in. They would be looking for security cameras in the neighbourhood, that was a given, but whether they would show anything? That was a question Frank didn't want to have the answer be no.

Frank walked back towards the waiting room, the door swishing closed behind him. He was torn. Eilis and Declan were at the point that they needed someone with them all the time. Only he didn't know who to call. He had reached out to Abe Finlay, knowing that Emma, Abe's wife, was working on this as she could. He had no idea how she found the people that she did. He had information from her that he needed to sort through but the opportunity had just not been there. He needed to do that in the next day or so.

Frank looked around as he heard footsteps, surprise on his face before his hand was out to shake that of the man standing in front of him.

"Richard? You're here?"

"I am. Abe called me and said that you needed a security team for the next couple of weeks. My team is available. I have put off what I had on the books to someone else. And we had a free week as well that we planned to use for training ourselves. You need our help more."

"We do. Listen, let's step out to the cafe, grab a coffee, and speak. I am waiting for the physician to finish his assessment on Declan."

Richard grinned, holding up a tray with two coffees.

"I planned ahead. What can you tell me?"

"Declan was beaten and left to die in his father's home. He was found tonight by his parents when they returned home from overseas. Eilis and Declan are engaged but Eilis is going through stuff."

"Stuff? So descriptive, that word." Richard laughed at Frank's grin. "Okay, my team is here. Two will be with Eilis and two with Declan. We'll try and keep his parents with Eilis as much as we can. But they'll be wanting to be at home too.

"They will. We'll work on that. I'm going to float between the two." Richard pointed towards Eilis, finding her watching them. "Eilis knows what's going on."

Frank nodded, his eyes on her.

"She does. I wish this had not happened. We just can't catch a break. Whoever it is, stays quite hidden although there are signs that they have been around. Eilis is getting ready to break free from the constraints and search for them herself."

"She will. She's the quiet one, the youngest one, but she's had enough. And with her fellow injured? She'll become a mother bear, ready to fight for him."

"That she will. Stay tight, Richard. I think the next couple of weeks will solve all this. The strange thing is that they are not receiving the packages, the messages, and whatnot that the victims usually do. They are not even being followed as far as we can determine."

"That means it's someone close to them." Richard's face grew grave. "We'll start sorting through everything for you, Frank. Go on. Talk to them."

Frank nodded once more before he dumped his coffee into a waste can and walked towards Eilis. He crouched down before her, a hand reaching for her and the other for Angela.

"Eilis? Angela? David? I know it's hard. I've seen Declan. He was going for imaging, Doc Wilson said. Then, we'll get you back with him."

"Thank you, Frank. Any word on who?" Eilis had had a chance to compose herself, the rigidity with which she was holding herself evident to those who knew her.

"Not yet, Eilis. We're working on that." Frank looked at the others, noting that Brinn and Darbi had appeared. If they were there, then Gareth and Flynn were somewhere around, more than likely with Ronan.

"How is he, Frank?" David could hardly speak, his worry that great.

"He's unconscious still, David. I don't know much past that. Doc can tell you better what has happened and his condition." Frank drew in a deep breath, his eyes narrowing for a moment. "Eilis? Angela? David? Richard is here for a reason. His team is here. For now, you will be under his protection. Two with you, Eilis, and two with Declan. Angela and David, we want to keep you with one or the other as much as we can. If you need to be away from them, we will have officers with you. We don't know how much someone would use you two to get to Declan. We don't have a sense yet of that."

"No, we don't, and at this point, you should. I want whoever it is and now." Eilis was angry, an anger that she knew she would have to surrender to God. She just couldn't at the moment.

"You're angry, Eilis." Frank nodded. "That's good." He shocked her with his words. "Your anger will help to keep you safe. You'll be on the look out for whoever it is and watching every single person. We'll solve this. I just wish it were today that we did."

Eilis nodded, her eyes on the woman sitting across from her.

———

"That woman, Frank? Sitting by herself? She has been intent on watching us. I have not seen her go back to see anyone or see anyone speaking with her."

Frank rose, knowing that Eilis had seen something. He walked away from her as if he was heading outdoors and stopped to study the room. He motioned to an officer. After a quick word with Frank, the officer approached the woman, spoke with her, and then escorted her out. They would be speaking with her. Frank prayed that she would have some answers for them.

Chapter 32

Angela's arm was around Eilis' shoulders and David's arm was around Angela's with his fingers touching Eilis. They were standing outside the door to Declan's room, waiting for the nurse to come for them. They were not sure yet about his condition but they were all praying for him to be awake and healing. They knew that hope was unlikely.

Doc Wilson stood behind them for a moment, studying the three of them. He had seen the imaging, the blood work, and done his own assessment. Declan was in difficulty, that much was obvious. He had been almost twenty-four hours without treatment, by their estimation. That meant he was in grave condition.

Eilis looked around, finding Doc near her.

"Doc Wilson? What can you tell us?" Hope was in her voice.

"Eilis. Angela. David. In you three go. We'll talk but for now go on in. I'll be right behind you." Doc Wilson had seen Frank heading his way.

"Doc?" Frank watched the three head for Declan, knowing that they would be there for a while. Richard headed past him, Stephen and Naomi trailing him.

"Frank? Whoever did this? Find them. If they get their hands on him again, he won't survive. Even now, it's touch and go."

Frank drew in a deep breath. This was not what he had wanted to hear.

"We'll have someone with him all the time and the same for Eilis and his parents. Richard, I think you know, and his team will be here."

"That's good. I'll get you a list of who is working with him. You'll want to vet them."

"I do. We need to. It would be easy for someone to get to him and we can't have that."

Eilis paused in her forward walk, her eyes on Declan. A hand went to her mouth as she choked back her tears. She could hear Angela struggling with her own emotions. David blinked rapidly. He had seen beatings like this overseas. He just never expected his son to be one in this condition.

Eilis reached for Declan's hand even as his mother reached for his other one. The two ladies stood on either side of the bed, their eyes on the young man both loved. David stood beside Angela, an arm around her. He looked around before he spoke quietly to a nurse. The nurse nodded, heading out to the waiting room.

"Ashlynn?"

Ashlynn looked up as the nurse stood in front of her and then she was on her feet.

"Declan?"

"David asked if you would come in and be with Eilis. She needs you."

Ashlynn followed the nurse, not sure what she was walking into but determined to do that for her niece. Eilis jumped as she felt her aunt's arm before she leaned against her. She could not take her eyes from Declan, seeing the bruising on his face but knowing that he was hurt and hurt badly.

Doc Wilson paused for a moment, nodding as he saw Ashlynn. It was only right, he decided, that she be there. Eilis needed her parents and they were not there. Ashlynn had become a mother to her and she was who Eilis needed.

He approached the four, his eyes on Declan before he moved to reassess him. He looked around, finding all eyes on him. He studied Eilis the longest, knowing what she had been through with the other ladies in her family.

"Eilis? Are you okay?" Doc Wilson's voice was calm and quiet in contrast to the beep and hiss of the equipment surrounding Declan.

Eilis shrugged, not sure what to say.

"I don't know, Doc. How am I to feel?" Her tears were falling into her heart, not onto her face.

"About like that. Angela and David? How are you two?" Doc watched as they didn't respond, simply shared a look with one another.

"What can you tell us?" David spoke for the group. His voice was ragged as he tried to control his emotions.

"As you know, he was beaten, sometime late yesterday afternoon. When was the last time anyone spoke with him?"

Eilis jumped, her eyes flying to Doc Wilson.

"That long ago? Is that why I couldn't get ahold of him? We talked around two. He was deep in work, he said."

Doc nodded.

"That's okay, Eilis. I'm just trying to get a sense of how long. Now as to his injuries? He has been beaten, as you can tell. Most of the blows were to his back and abdomen. His ribs are fractured on the left side. There was no damage to the lung, which is good. He does have internal bleeding which we can watch. We don't need to rush him into surgery, if that's what you're thinking. We monitor it and if necessary then we'll talk with you first. He does have a concussion, which is part of the reason that he has not roused. We're moving him to a room on the medical floor shortly. Until then, you four can stay with him. I understand Richard and his team will be around for the next while. We're fine with that. We'll limit who gets in to him."

"If we need to hire a nurse to special for him, Doc, we'll do that." David shared a look with Doc and then Richard, who nodded. That had been Richard's thought and suggestion to Frank.

"We'll see, David. For now, I'm off to see another patient. I'll be around. The nurse will be in and out over the next while. If you need anything, ask."

173

Doc Wilson walked away, pausing to tilt his head back. His heart was raised in prayer for that group and particularly for Declan. He was not rousing and that concerned him. He was afraid that there were more serious injuries than he had determined.

Eilis turned to watch Doc walk away, finding Richard's eyes on her. She sighed. *Her freedom just walked away, didn't it? When will this be over, Lord? Who is it?*

Ashlynn moved away at last, knowing that she had to speak with the others. She hesitated at the doorway before she straightened up and walked towards the waiting room. Naomi paced beside her, something that Ashlynn was grateful for.

Chani looked up as Ashlynn appeared, on her feet and in her aunt's arms. Brinn and Darbi were close by. Ashlynn could see the three men watching from just behind her girls. This was difficult, she acknowledged. She could the coughs and sneezes from those waiting to be seen, the quiet conversations between people, the odd chiming or ringing of a phone. It seemed surreal to her, to be doing this for the fourth time. When would it end?

Chapter 33

"Aunt Ash?" Chani stood back for a moment, her eyes shifting between her aunt and the door. "Is he worse?"

"No, he's not worse, dear. He's still unconscious. They're moving him to a room soon, Doc Wilson said."

"That's good, right?" Brinn moved in on her aunt before she sought Gareth's arms.

"It is. He has internal injuries, fractured ribs, and a concussion. No surgery as yet, he said." Ashlynn felt weak all of a sudden and felt Flynn and Ronan there to help her to a seat. "I'm sorry. I don't know why I did that."

"It's okay, Aunt Ash." Darbi was there, holding out a bottle of orange juice. "It happens. Our bodies do that." She looked around, not being anyone that she would suspect. "What do we do to help?"

"That I don't know, dear. I really don't know. For now, we pray for them. I'll stay tonight but I have to be at work tomorrow."

Brinn chewed at her lip.

"So do I. I can't not walk the dogs."

Chani shrugged.

"I'll be here. Darbi?"

"I can be here in the afternoon. What about her shop? Hasn't Sally retired?"

"She has. I spoke with her earlier. She'll go in and help for now. She offered before I could even ask. Now, let's spend some time in prayer for our family. We need that."

Late that night, Eilis curled up in a chair in the waiting room. She simply refused to leave. She knew that Angela and David were around, David apparently heading off to see if he could find something for them to eat. She wasn't hungry but knew that she had to. Her phone out, Eilis scrolled through her messages, a sad look on her face. This was not what she had expected. This was to be a happy time for them. Only it wasn't. Declan was hurt, likely because of her. She sent off a quick text to Sally, just confirming the work for the next day. She didn't think that she would be there.

Angela's head was back on the wall, her eyes closed. She was almost asleep, the travel and the worry taking their toll. She needed to sleep but she also needed to pray. Sleep won at last. David sat beside her, a hand resting on hers before he looked over at Eilis, finding her sleeping as well.

Stephen and Naomi walked around the halls, the nurses accepting that they had to be there. They too were deeply worried about Declan and also Eilis. Eilis they had gotten to know somewhat but she was still a mystery.

Naomi paused for a moment, sensing something off. She turned and watched as a man walked away. She followed him to the main floor and then to the door. Her phone was out as she took his photo and then a photo of the car he jumped into. She searched her photos and grinned. She had managed to snap the license plate. She sent it off to Frank, knowing that he would want it. She didn't expect a response until the next day

Naomi stopped beside Stephen, a quiet word to him before she sent him the photos as well as sending them off to the other three on the team. If the man showed up again then he would be detained. That was a given, she thought.

Early in the morning, Eilis roused, on her feet and heading for Declan. Her tears had dried up overnight and she could not cry any more, she thought. She stood beside Declan's bed, watching for him to move and not seeing that. Her hand rested on his cheek, feeling the stubble on it. She prayed as she hadn't prayed before, begging God to let Declan awake. Then her prayer changed and she had to release Declan to God's will. Eilis also prayed that she would be that lamp here that God wanted her to be, to be that light for Him.

Richard walked towards her, his steps sounding almost too loud in the quiet. Eilis tense and then relaxed. It had to be someone who meant her no harm, she thought.

"Eilis? How is he?"

"I don't know, Richard. He's not moving and he's not waking up. How is he to be?" Eilis opened her mouth to apologize for the bite in her words, snapping it closed as Richard shook his head.

"It's okay, Eilis. I understand that you are frustrated and worried. I would be too." Richard looked around for a moment. "Listen, I need to show you a photo."

"You do?" Eilis frowned as she studied the man. "I know him. He has a business near mine. A tobacco shop. Is he the one?"

Richard shrugged as she looked up at him.

"I don't know, Eilis. He was around last night when no one should have been. Naomi snapped this photo. I'm sure that she sent it on to Frank."

"Of course, she did. He'll be around soon too, won't he?" Eilis was frustrated, to say the least. "When does this end?"

"Soon, we pray, Eilis. Frank is working as best he can, considering all the cases that he has on his desk. Emma is working this as well. I spoke with her last night. Abe is sending some of his men this way in the next day or so with what she has. We need to keep you safe."

"And what about Angela and David? Don't you have to keep them safe too?" Eilis was worried about them.

"We will. But you are our priority. It may mean that we rush you away from here without any notice. Expect that. Have one of your family pack a bag for you that they can give to one of us. David is doing that for Declan as well." Richard watched with compassion as her eyes closed and a single tear trickled down her cheek.

"Will he be alive to use it?"

"We pray that he will. It is surprising how quickly someone can bounce back from a beating, once God becomes involved in the healing. It may not work out that way for Declan, but that is how we are praying for him. And for you."

Eilis could barely whisper a thank you through her blocked throat before she turned back to Declan, her hand on his. She prayed as she had not prayed before, filling her prayer with every promise that she could think of.

Chapter 34

Declan began to move early that afternoon, pain evident on his face as he did so. He could hear someone calling his name. It sounded so much like his mother but it couldn't be. They were overseas. He felt the hand on his cheek and leaned into it. He didn't know who it was. He only knew that he felt comfort from the touch. A lady, he decided, and not his mother.

The physician who had taken on his care studied his chart and then him. He frowned. There was no way that Declan should be rousing. Not with the injuries he suffered, he thought. He turned away for a moment, catching Richard watching him, a slight smile on his face.

"Doc?" Richard spoke quietly.

"He's rousing, Richard, is it? He shouldn't be." The physician was puzzled.

"He is, Doc. That's God at work. He's healing through God's touch." Richard held up a hand as the physician opened his mouth. "I've seen it many times before."

"I have too. When you work in modern medicine, you forget who the Great Healer is. If he keeps waking up and stays awake, we'll see about letting him go in the next couple of days. You have somewhere to hide him, I gather."

"We do. But he'll want to go home. Or his parents will want him at their place."

"And Eilis, his fiancée? Where will she be?" The physician gave a small smirk at the grin on Richard's face.

"With him. That's a given, as they say, Doc." Richard turned as he heard footsteps and walked away to greet Frank.

"Richard? Has that man been around?" Frank wasted no time with pleasantries.

"Not that we have seen. I hear that his place is being watched."

"That's what I'm hearing." Frank didn't acknowledge that Pat was doing that, having taken on the task without saying a word. "How's Declan?"

"He's starting to rouse. Doc thinks if he awakens and stays awake we can take him out of here in the next couple of days."

"That would help. It would make it easier to guard them." Frank was frustrated at the pace of the case. He really had no good leads or suspects and that was so unusual.

"Eilis will want to work." Richard had talked with Eilis and knew her wishes.

"I know that she will. We'll figure it out somehow. It doesn't seem to matter where they are, does it?" Frank sighed as his phone chimed. Excusing himself, he walked away, not seeing Eilis approaching.

"Where's he off to?" Eilis stopped beside Richard, a frown on her face. She felt that was all she was doing lately, frowning.

———

“He had a call. Did the doc talk with you?”

“He did. Declan is rousing more and more. Where do we go, Richard? I need to be in the shop. Sally has plans for next week. I won’t ask her to change them.”

“We’ll figure it out. We have come to the conclusion that it won’t work to hide you two away. There hasn’t been enough information come in to tell us who the bad guy is as you call him.”

“Or bad girl. And which one of us are they after? Have you figured that out? They could have gone after me to get to Declan. Or did they go after us to get to his parents? That’s been done before.”

“We know that, Eilis. We’re looking at everything that we can, trying to figure it all out. Now, where are you going?” Richard watched with slight amusement as Eilis paced in a circle around him.

Eilis shrugged.

“I have no idea. I would like to get outside for a bit, if I could.” She looked up at him with hope on her face.

Richard handed her the jacket that she had dropped on a chair.

“Then, that’s what we do. We’ll go find ourselves a hot drink, something to nibble on, and then find somewhere outside to sit. It’s warm out there today.”

“I know. It’s the type of day that I like to be outside. I just wish it was different.” Eilis didn’t continue her words, not wanting to express how she really felt.

Richard nodded, knowing that she was afraid and frustrated too. Everyone who they protected reached that point. That point was when they tried to run. Only, Eilis wouldn't be doing that. She just would not leave Declan.

David approached them, his own cup of coffee in his hand, and sat beside Eilis. Angela had been in touch, bringing him back to the hospital. He had been up to see his son, finding him still rousing, his eyes opening and closing. He then had hunted for Eilis, needing to see for himself that she was okay.

"David? Have you seen Declan?" Eilis reached to hug him.

"I have. He's rousing more and more, isn't he?" David reached to give her a one-armed hug, knowing that she would be a beloved part of their family soon.

"He is. I'm sorry." Eilis refused to look at either man.

Richard and David shared a look. David was puzzled at her words. Richard had heard them many times before from the victims.

"Sorry? For what?" David sipped at his coffee as he waited for Eilis to respond.

Eilis hesitated to speak. She listened to the sound of traffic from a nearby road and the sound of vehicles passing nearby in the parking lot. She really had no idea why she was sorry. She just felt that she had to apologize.

———

Shrugging, Eilis finally spoke. Her voice was low and broken.

"For this. For Declan getting hurt. It should have happened. I brought this to him."

"No, I don't think that you did." Richard spoke at last, his eyes full of compassion as he watched her.

"I must have. This would not have happened had Declan and I not met. He would not have been hurt." Eilis tried to rise but couldn't, finding David's arm around her shoulders.

"I doubt that this is your fault. In fact, I know it's not." David watched her face as she refused to look at him. "If you had been in danger when you met Declan, he would have stepped in no matter who you were. You are now a beloved member of our family. We hold no blame towards you, Eilis. Declan has made his choice in choosing you to be his helpmeet for life. Now, we just need to get him well and solve this."

Eilis had turned her head to study him, finally nodding at his words. She blinked back tears, knowing that David was correct, that whoever had been in danger would have had Declan stepping in.

Chapter 35

Declan's eyes opened at last and stayed open. He grimaced as he moved his head, his eyes searching the room. A hospital bed? What did he do? He didn't think that he had done anything to merit this. He groaned as he shifted, feeling battered and bruised. A hand reached to touch his face and he leaned into it.

Eilis Davidt to kiss Declan's cheek, her free hand reaching for his. Declan's hand tightened on hers before he looked around, blinking to clear his eyes.

"Do I know you?" Declan was puzzled for a moment.

"You do, Declan. I'm Eilis. We're engaged." Eilis continued to Davidd over him, not seeing the woman who had paused at the doorway, a dark look on her face and hatred showing in her eyes. Eilis' sole focus was on Declan and him alone.

"We are? I don't remember." Declan drew in a deep breath, the pain hitting for a moment. "What happened?"

"You were beaten up, Declan, and left to die." Eilis knew that he would want only the truth.

"I was? Is that why I hurt?"

"It is." Eilis watched as Timothy approached her. "We're under protection, Declan. The doctor said that you could leave in a day or so. That is, if you could stay awake."

"I can." Declan frowned at her and then at Timothy. "When can I leave?"

"Not right now. The nurse is on her way in and the doctor is too." Timothy reached to touch Eilis' arm. "We need to talk, Eilis, and now."

Eilis spun, anger sparking from her.

"I am not leaving. Not right now. Not when Declan has just awakened."

Declan stared in awe at her. He had not seen her like this, at least, he didn't think that he had.

Timothy simply shook his head and with a hand on her arm drew her from the room, nodding at the nurse as she passed them.

"We need to move you two and move you soon. There was someone watching you just a couple of minutes ago."

"There was?" Eilis sighed. "That's what they do, isn't it?"

"It is. Now, Richard is setting up a place for you."

"I'm not going anywhere but to my home. The same for Declan. He'll want to go to his home. And that is going to be so difficult for him. Will his parents go there?"

"That's what we thought that you would say. For now, we're putting all four of you at Declan's. We'll get you back and forth to your work. As of now, you have a new employee. Silver stays with you during the day. Stephen will be with Declan. At night, Naomi and I will be there. Richard will float as to where he needs to be." Timothy was not backing down from her. He had been through this too many times to do that.

Eilis had listened to him, her eyes on the people in the waiting room. She sighed.

"That's about what I thought you would say. And that woman in the seat near the door? She doesn't like me. Never has. And I have no idea why. Is she the one?"

Timothy had been watching her, knowing that she had been the one in the doorway just a few moments ago. He watched as two officers approached her, spoke with her, and then had her walk away with them. Eilis was shocked.

"What just happened?"

"I reported her. Frank has made sure that there are officers around here for the next day or so. I just asked them to speak with her. We'll find out why she feels that way."

Eilis shrugged, her mind already moving on to something else. She needed her family right about then and didn't have them. And she refused to ask for them to come. Eilis didn't realize that she was withdrawing from them in an effort to protect them. Only, that would never work. She should have known that from what the other three had gone through.

Timothy turned her back towards Declan's room. He knew that was where she wanted to be but he also knew that he had to reach out to Richard.

Richard stood in Frank's office an hour later, a troubled look on his face. To hear that someone had been that close to the couple, even though they were under guard? That was disturbing. And then to hear that the woman was a business owner in town? One who ran a towing company? That was even more disturbing. They needed to make a connection between her and Eilis and Declan and that just wasn't obvious. Not as yet.

Frank turned from his computer. He had been searching for information on a case and had simply waved Richard in. He had shot him a keen glance before he apologized for continuing his work.

"Richard? You're here?" Frank shifted on his chair, watching as Richard finally sat.

"I am. I hear that someone was brought in from the hospital. Someone who had been very close to Declan and Eilis."

Frank nodded slowly. He could not say much, not and endanger the investigation.

"That's correct. I understand that it was one of your men who spotted her."

"It was. Where do we put them, Frank?"

"We're not going to be able to hide them away. Neither will let us do that. What are your plans?"

Richard snorted, bringing a grin to Frank's face.

"We had plans, but this may change those. We had planned to keep the four all together at Declan's."

"That would work. He has a house that you can set up security around without difficulty. His neighbours have good security cameras. David and Angela will want to be at their house though."

"They will. They have already expressed that wish. We can do that."

Frank nodded, knowing that Richard would have weighed the risks and made his decision

"Don or Abe coming in?"

"Don is. Abe is away for the next few days. Emma's sending you information I gather from what Abe let drop."

"More than likely. I haven't had a chance to get to whatever is here." Frank rose and walked out with Richard. "We'll pick up where we can. That's not a problem."

"We know that, Frank. Perhaps one of your lady cops would be willing to go into Eilis' shop. Naomi or Silver will be there but an extra set of eyes would be good."

"I can arrange that. Let me know if you need anything."

Frank watched as Richard walked away, a slump to his shoulders that was not normally there. *Bless my friend, dear Lord. He's hurting and bearing a burden. He's young yet but has seen too much of life. It's weighing down his soul.*

Frank stood for a moment, his face tilted to the sky, his eyes closed. This case was weighing on them all. They could not get a sense of why or who. But just maybe, he thought, this arrest would be the catalyst to solving this. But then there was the issue with what the ladies had received. He had spoken with the investigator in their home town. They were both puzzled as to why. Frank's prayer was that it wasn't to go after Ashlynn but that was his deep-felt conviction.

Chapter 36

Eilis wandered her apartment the next evening. Declan had been discharged and taken home to his parents' place. She had been there until just a bit ago when she felt that she had to come home. Something was telling her to do that. Eilis had learned over the years to follow those nudgings, something her father would have told her was God speaking to her.

Silver watched from where she was working at the kitchen counter. The apartment had an open floor plan, the kitchen open to the living room. She sighed to herself. This is where it got difficult, she knew. Timothy was downstairs in the shop, a cot set up for him. Eilis had insisted on that. He had shaken his head, simply stating that he would be on guard all night. She had frowned at him and simply moved the cot downstairs on her own.

"Eilis? Here. Have a sandwich. You haven't eaten yet." Silver walked towards her, her socked feet padding softly on the wooden floor. She handed her the plate and mug that she held before she was back with her own mug of tea.

"Thank you, Silver. I need this, don't I?" Eilis curled up in her favourite chair, staring at the floor. "Has there been any word that you know of?"

"Not that I am aware of. Richard will hold a briefing with us in the morning. That's what he does. Then we hand off to Stephen and Naomi. There is another team with Declan."

"Don, isn't it? I had met him in the past. Where's Abe and his team?" Eilis smirked as she asked that and then bit into her sandwich, chewing thoughtfully before she swallowed. "I haven't heard from Emma. I thought that I would have."

"I understand that Abe's team has been away. Emma? She's working it. I hear that she's heading this way with some friends in the next day or so."

"She is? Oh, wonderful! Did she say who?"

"No, she didn't. I can ask if you like." Silver reached for her phone, pausing as Eilis shook her head.

"No, it's okay. Whoever comes is welcome." Eilis grew quiet, staring at her mug, her thoughts troubled.

Silver watched her, knowing that the time had arrived for it to become very dangerous for Eilis. Her prayer was that they would be able to protect her and keep her safe. They had had people hurt who they were protecting but had never lost anyone. She prayed that this would not be the one time that they did.

Rising, Silver headed for the stairs, intent on finding Timothy. He was standing just inside the back door, listening intently. A hand raised stopped Silver, who reached for her weapon.

Stephen pointed to the front. Silver nodded and headed that way. She could hear the soft rattling of the doorknob as someone tried it. She paused, letting her eyes become used to the low light. She watched as the dark figure moved away, to meet up with another dark figure. She paced back towards Stephen.

———

"There were two out front." Her voice was barely audible.

"There's another one here at the back. He's been trying the door." Stephen looked around, not sure where they could hide. "There are two staircases?"

"There are. One leads down here. The other to the outside. We'd never make it that way." Silver drew in a deep breath. "Now what, Stephen?"

"I sent a text to Richard. He's on his way and is sending help. Only I don't know that we'll be safe until then." Stephen pointed to the stairs. "Up there, Silver. We'll lock the door down here and then wait at the other outside door. Hopefully we'll get a chance to escape."

Eilis looked up in alarm as Silver and then Stephen flew up the stairs, the door closed and bolted behind them.

"Silver? Stephen?" She was on her feet, a hand to her throat, fear coursing through her.

"Get your jacket and boots, Eilis. We may need to flee from here." Silver reached to turn down even more lights. "Quick. Down the stairs to the other door. We may need to leave on the run. There are men outside your shop."

Eilis stared at Silver for a moment before reaching for her jacket, slipped on her boots, and pocketed her phone. She followed Stephen down the stairs, Silver coming down behind them, having locked the door behind her.

———

They waited, Stephen with his ear to the door. He could heard the footsteps out there as the men moved around the back doors. He felt the doorknob twisting under his hand. It didn't open. Stephen moved slightly, feeling the restlessness that Eilis was exhibiting. He couldn't take a chance on opening the door.

Silver felt her phone vibrating and pulled it out. She breathed a sigh of relief. Richard was outside with Naomi and Timothy. Patrol officers were there as well. All they had to do was stay where they were and he would come and find them. She tapped Stephen's shoulder, handing him her phone.

Stephen read the text and frowned. That didn't sound like Richard. He shook his head at Silver, pointing to the phone number. She frowned and realized what Stephen had seen. The message was not from Richard. She sent another text message to Richard, receiving his quick response. How long was what he asked? Were they safe? He would find them, sending patrol officers in the meanwhile.

Eilis shifted on her feet, her eyes moving from Stephen to Silver. Something was off, she knew, and that meant danger to all three of them. She began to pray, begging God to protect them. She screamed as the door suddenly flew open. Stephen stumbled out, going down under a blow from a bat. Silver grabbed for her hand, pulling her with her as she began to run, seeking somewhere for them to hide.

Eilis stumbled as she moved forward, her feet not functioning as they should. She gave a scream as a man appeared in front of them, a hand out for her arm.

She jerked it away, finding themselves suddenly surrounded. There were coarse shouts behind them before Eilis and Silver disappeared, leaving Stephen in a sprawled heap near the now swinging door and patrol officers moving in on the men who had attempted the abduction.

Richard knelt beside Stephen, a hand to his back before he was on his feet, searching for Eilis and Silver. They were not outside. Patrol officers moved into the building, not finding them either. Richard stared at the three men now standing with their hands cuffed behind them. He knew them. His heart fell. This was way worth than he thought it was. These men were hired guns, and whoever they were after usually didn't survive. How Eilis and Silver had managed to escape would be a tale to hear he knew. He turned as he heard his voice called.

"Richard? What happened?" Frank stopped beside him, watching the commotion around him.

"Silver sent a text. Someone was trying to get in. I have no idea what happened here." Richard turned in a circle, feeling eyes on them. "Someone is watching us."

Frank nodded, having seen Pat in the shadows.

"A friend is for sure. Hang tight, Richard. We'll talk with him." Frank walked away even as Timothy and Naomi approached him.

"Richard? What happened?" Timothy pointed towards Stephen.

———

"We're not sure. Timothy, you're with him. Naomi, Richard has someone for us to talk to. Right now, Eilis and Silver are missing."

Chapter 37

Pat backed away deeper into the shadows as he watched the activity near Eilis' shop. He knew that the two ladies were safe. He had seen to that himself. He had them hidden not too far away from here, ready to come back when the activity settled down. He sighed to himself. This was not what he expected to have happen but he should have.

Frank finally was able to walk towards Richard. He rubbed at his head. Silver and Eilis had disappeared that much was evident. Stephen was still unconscious so he couldn't question him.

"Frank?" Richard's voice brought Frank's head up.

"Richard? Okay, let's walk. I think I know where they are." Frank pointed towards where Pat had appeared.

Richard shared a look with the other two and then walked beside Frank, his steps slowing as he saw Pat. He shot a look at Frank and then back at Pat.

"Pat?" Frank slowed to a stop, his eyes searching around him.

"I have the ladies, Frank. For now, they're safe. Eilis doesn't know anything. Silver has a tale to tell you."

Frank nodded before he turned to Richard, who simply shook his head.

"Okay, Pat. Take us to them. It will be a while before they can come back but they should be able to be back here tonight or early in the morning." Frank paced beside Pat, knowing that Pat would have tucked the ladies somewhere close.

Eilis spun as she heard footsteps approaching, finding Silver in front of her with her weapon drawn. Silver drew in a deep breath of relief.

"Richard? Stephen?" Silver was afraid to ask how he was.

"He's unconscious, Silver, but alive. I'll head in to check on him. Right now, Frank needs to talk with you too."

"Of course he does." Eilis moved forward and around Silver. "Frank?"

"Eilis?" He gave a brief grin before he sobered. "I hear that you didn't see much. Now, we'll get you home soon. We'll do that. Silver?"

Silver spoke quickly, simply stating what she had observed until the time that they were whisked away.

Frank nodded, having felt that was what had happened. Pat moved forward, handing out water bottles for them all. Eilis slumped onto a table that stood nearby, fatigue evident. She had not slept much in the last couple of days.

"Declan? He's safe?" Eilis refused to look up, finding Frank beside her.

"He is, Eilis. I made sure of that. Don has been in touch." Frank waited patiently for Eilis to respond, knowing just how close to collapse that she had to be.

Eilis finally nodded, her eyes hardly able to stay open.

"That's good to hear. When can I see Declan?"

Frank caught her as she collapsed, heading for the pallet that Pat pointed to. He laid her gently down, stepping away as Silver moved in to cover her.

"It had to come, Frank." Pat paced away from them and back. "She's been running on nerve, trying to work, be with her family, to be that light she always talks about."

"That she has." Frank paced as well before he turned. "Richard, I have to head out. Stay with Pat. He'll help you get the ladies home. I put in a call to Don. He's good where he is. Update me on Stephen when you get word."

Richard watched Frank walk away, knowing just how dangerous this had become. He had no idea if he could keep Eilis safe. It had been taken to a different level that night, with them trying to gain entrance to her very home. He would have to go back over that building, tightening up the security. He had thoughts about the shop but he wasn't sure that Eilis would go for them.

"Richard? What do we do about her work? She won't quit." Naomi paced over to him, worry on her face. This was unusual for her. She never usually showed her feelings when they were in work mode.

"I know, Naomi. I can't see that we can block the back from the front. There is a door there that we can fix with a strong lock but I don't know that she would have time to slam it shut and lock it."

"I doubt it. The back door can be kept locked. This is putting her staff at risk. They're willing to stay but I know Eilis well enough to know that she's worried about them."

"We have one of you ladies with her. Frank promised to bring in a female officer. Let me talk to him and see what we can come up with. If we have to pay for the staff to stay home for a few days, we'll do that. Barnabas Carey called me this afternoon, having caught wind of what's going on. He's offered to provide funding for that."

"He has? That's wonderful. Now, if we can solve this, it would be great." Silver had walked up as well, listening to the conversation.

They all turned as Eilis spoke from beside them.

"He would do that? I have heard of him and the Barnabas Foundation. I think that I'll need to let the ladies take some time. I don't want them hurt." A troubled look stayed on her face even as she prayed through what she needed to do. "Richard? You research things. I know that from Darbi. I need you to look up someone for me without it going to Frank or even with Darbi working it. I think that I know who is behind it all."

Richard studied her, seeing the worry and fear on her face. He sighed. She's gone and done it, he thought.

"Who is it, Eilis?" He waited patiently for her to recover her composure. When she didn't, he asked again.

"Who is it?" Eilis named someone, someone they had not considered at all.

"Them?" Richard was surprised at the very least.

"Them." Eilis prayed as she confirmed that. She had not wanted it to be them but the conviction was growing that it was them.

Pat spoke from behind her, having come to the same conclusion that day.

"I agree with Eilis. They have fingers in too many spots in the town. Word on the street is that she has crossed the line and is looking for an assassin. Only no one is taking her up on that. She may have found someone from out of town."

Richard's movement froze as he stared at Eilis and then Pat.

"Eilis?" His voice was low and hard.

Pat nodded, confirming Richard's supposition.

"Eilis. As to why, we're working on that. It has nothing to do with her shop. That much we know. We think that Eilis may have heard something or seen something years ago and not remembered it, or if she did, not counted it as of much value."

Eilis stared at Pat in shock.

"I did? I don't remember being around her or him at all."

"It may have been when you were out somewhere, Eilis, somewhere so routine that you didn't pay attention to those around you. We all do that at times. We're so concerned with what we're doing that people around us are inconsequential."

Chapter 38

Declan paced his home, coming to stand at his desk, staring down at the work piled there. He needed to work but just didn't want to. He hurt too much and was too worried about his lady. He sat, reaching for the envelopes, opening them and then sorting out the mail. There were letters that needed answering right then. Declan opened his word processing to do so.

Three hours later, Don came to find him, sitting down across from him. He simply waited for Declan to acknowledge that he was there. While he waited, Don prayed for him and for his lady, knowing that the crisis was building for them.

Looking up at last, Declan sat back, his pen dropping to the desktop.

"How long have you been there, Don?"

"Not long. You were deep in your work." Don reached to help fold the letters and stuff the envelopes. "I'll have one of the fellows mail these for you. Now, what do we do with you? You need to rest."

"I know. I just had to check to see where my work stands and let my clients know that I have been sidelined. I sent out emails this afternoon." Declan rubbed at his face, not wanting to ask but knowing that he had to. "Have you heard how Eilis is?"

"She's fine. She and Silver had an adventure last night that left Stephen injured." Don's hand went up. "She is okay, Declan. She was gotten away and kept safe. She's at work right now. We'll get you two together later. Your parents are out and about, your father said. They had things that they needed to do."

"They did. They're back here permanently, Mom said. I'm glad. I worried about them so much."

"And they worried about you. They are worried now about both you and Eilis."

"They are. I just don't know who it would be." Declan frowned at the look on Don's face. "Don? Have there been developments?"

"There have been. Richard contacted me this morning and we have been doing some research. Your lady gave Frank a name."

"And it is?" Declan waited almost impatiently.

"She did." Don gave the names, causing Declan to sit back in disbelief.

"Them? How did she do that?"

"We don't know, but Frank and Pat agreed apparently. Frank is looking into that. Eilis has asked Richard to do the same. I understand that's what he's been doing today. And Emma has come up with the same couple."

"Okay, then. How do we prove it? And can we?" Declan was hopeful that this would soon be over.

"We can. And it is being worked on even as we speak. Apparently Darbi and the other ladies were talking and came up with the same name. Darbi investigating it. She's pulled in Garrett as well."

"That's good. And now has Ronan's cousin weighed in as well as his friends?"

Don began to laugh, knowing that they had. He was on his feet and heading for the door.

"Come on, Declan. You need to eat. And you need your pain medications whether you want them or not."

Declan levered himself to his feet, waiting until he felt that he could move properly before he followed Don. He was exhausted but he was determined to stay on his feet to help find whoever it was. His lady was at risk and in danger and he wanted to end that. With God's help, he would do that, even if it cost his life.

Eilis turned that afternoon, finding Silver standing near her. Silver grinned at her before nodding towards the door to the front of the shop.

"Eve is enjoying herself. Watch out. You may find yourself with a new employee."

"She would do that?" Eilis stepped to where she could watch Eve for a moment. "She's picked it up really quickly."

"She has. Listen, I spoke with Richard a few moments ago. He's heading Declan's way later today. For some reason, he wanted to know if you would like to go."

"What? How can he even ask that? What time?"

"Once you've closed the shop and cleaned up, he'll be around. And yes, Stephen will be here. He's better."

"I am so glad. It scared me when he went down and didn't move." Eilis stared at the carnations that she was holding in her hand. "I think that we can close up now. It's near enough." She looked around as Eve spoke.

"Thank you, Eilis, for letting me work here. I really enjoyed it."

"Is that a hint that you want to retire and come work for me?" Eilis grinned at her vigorous nod. "Think about it. I need to hire and train someone to take over for me now that I've taken on Sally's role. Dee wants to stay out front."

"You mean that? I'll pray about it. My husband and I want me to find something safer. Although this place doesn't seem so safe." Eve grinned at the other two ladies laughed before she walked away.

Silver locked up the front of the store, watching as Eilis rang off the cash and then headed for the workroom to lock it into the safe.

Angela turned as she felt a hand on her back and simply reached to hug Eilis. She studied the young lady, before she simply Davidt her head and prayed for her.

"Angela?" Eilis spoke quietly, her eyes on the other lady.

"I'm okay, Eilis. And you?"

Eilis nodded, hearing the sounds of many voices.

"Who all is here?"

"We are. Your family. Some of Don's men. Richard's team. And Garrett."

"Oh, good. Then we can start working. I closed the shop tomorrow. It's Saturday but I needed a full two days to try and recover. Are you and David heading back to your home?”

"Not for now. We're staying with Declan. And I would gather that you will be too. I see that bag Silver is trying hard to hide."

Chapter 39

Declan rose from his chair close to midnight that night, stretching and then groaning with the pain he felt. The pain was not as severe as it had been but it was still there. He walked away from his office, leaving the men there staring after him before exchanging glances. They went back to their research, quiet conversation among them.

Eilis raised her head as Declan walked away before she too rose and followed him. Her hand on his back had him turning towards her and wrapping her into his arms. They stood for a few moments before she moved them to the couch and then down on it. Declan sat, his arm around his lady, a thoughtful look on his face.

"Declan? What are you thinking about?" Eilis studied him, seeing the pain in his face. She was up and away, back with a bottle of water and his medications. "You need to take these."

Declan nodded as he swallowed the pills, knowing that he would be asleep soon.

"Have we made any progress, sweetheart?" Declan thought that they had but wasn't sure.

"We have, love. We have. The fellows will correlate it all and pass it on to Frank. He was in and out a couple of hours ago on his way home."

"He was? I missed that." Declan sighed, his eyes closing for a moment. "You're okay?"

"I am. I was so scared but Pat got us to safety." Eilis snuggled down against Declan, feeling his body starting to relax. "Will we solve this, Declan?"

"I am sure that we will. Emma came through, once more, with information for us. That will help. She said that she had passed it on to Frank."

"Frank is wearing out, you know. He's so busy."

"He is. They're short an investigator, I know, and that doesn't help." Declan's eyes closed and he slept, his head against Eilis'.

Eilis sat for a while before she rose, tucking a blanket around Declan. She walked back to the office, to stand in the doorway and watch. Ronan rose and came towards her.

"Eilis? What are you thinking?"

"Me? Thinking? I'm trying not to, you know. My thoughts are too scary." She smirked at him as he laughed. "Come with me, Ronan, and tell me what you've found. You all need fresh coffee and some food."

Ashlynn turned from where she had been working at the counter, simply reaching to hug her niece. She knew that the end of the adventure, as it was termed, was close, and this was a difficult time for them all.

"Eilis?"

"They need to eat, Aunt Ash." Eilis peeked at the counter. "Oh, wonderful! You've made food."

"Yes, Angela and I have. Now, Ronan, head on in with the first tray and then come back." Ashlynn watched her niece closely, a frown on her face. There was a peace about Eilis tonight that hadn't been there. Ashlynn sighed herself, knowing that Eilis had reached a decision. Whether she would tell them or not, that was the question.

Early morning found the men rising, heading off for their day's work. Eilis paused as she close the door, knowing that this day would be it. She could feel that this would be the day that they were approached, threatened, and the culprits arrested. She could never explain it afterwards when she was asked. Eilis simply said that God had spoken to her, to prepare her. She stood on the porch, her eyes on the sky as the dawn was breaking, relishing the colours and praying that she would live to see another day.

Naomi approached her, turning her back into the house. Pat had reached out to Richard, warning him of the rumours on the streets. Richard had simply agreed that the time to break this case wide open had happened.

The sound of a car door quietly closing had Naomi shoving Eilis into the house and closing and locking the door. She watched through the window, seeing a man and woman approaching them. Eilis had protested at the sudden move but grew quiet as Naomi had held up a hand.

The door opened under Naomi's hand to let the couple in. Dave and Rylee Allison stood there, not sure of what was happening.

"Dave?" Eilis moved to where she could see him. "You're here? Let me guess. Emma sent you two."

Dave grinned even as Rylee moved to hug Eilis.

"She did. We can't stay for long, but she wanted us to come and see you, to bring you what she has. She's confirmed your suspicions and found more people involved than what you said."

"She has?" Eilis drew in a deep breath. "That's about what I thought she would find. Come on in. Declan is still sleeping. Timothy is around about outside. Richard is tied up somewhere with another call."

Eilis listened carefully as Dave spoke, Rylee watching Eilis. Eilis was near breaking, Rylee decided, having gone through something similar herself.

"So, Eilis, what can we do now?" Dave, a paramedic, had been assessing her as well.

"I have no idea. This has helped. Your notes and Emma's will certainly explain it all to Declan. I haven't had the heart to awaken him yet. And his parents did finally crash somewhere around two I think. Everyone else is away at work. They're planning on coming back tonight to continue their research."

"Somehow, you don't think that will happen, do you?" Rylee reached to hug her. "You think it will all be over by then."

"I do. I have that confidence from God that it will be. I don't get those feelings very often but when I do, they are usually right. Declan and I need to head your way at some point."

"Do that." Rylee stood, hugging Eilis once more, before they walked to the door. "I left you some of our baking from the Irish bakeshop. Enjoy."

"We will." Eilis grinned at her, accepted the hug from Dave, and then watched as they drove away. She turned back into the house, pensive in mood, as she tidied the kitchen and then took mugs of coffee to head for the living room.

Declan was stirring, not quite awake. At some point, he had stretched out on the couch, pain driving him deeper into sleep. He could hear movement around him and felt Eilis touch on his head before he slept once more.

Eilis curled up in a nearby chair, the notes from Emma on her knee. She wasn't reading them. Instead, she was communing with her Lord, drawing from His strength for the day, a day that she both feared and yet wanted to happen.

Chapter 40

Rousing in the early afternoon, Declan raised himself to a sitting position, his head in his hands for a moment. His headache pounded for a moment before it subsided to a dull roar as he phrased it. He rubbed at his forehead, frowning. Something was off, he could sense. Only he had no idea what. He looked up, ready to rise before his motions stopped. Declan stared at the man sitting across from him. He had no idea who he was or how he managed to get into his house.

Declan could hear no movement in the house and that scared him. There should be. He knew that his mother and Eilis had planned to stay all day as had Richard's team.

"Who are you?" Declan spoke at last, not taking his eyes from the man.

"Not important. On your feet." The man was on his feet, a weapon pointed directly at Declan's head.

Declan froze for a moment. Then he rose, not taking his eyes from the man.

"Where do I go?"

"That way. To that room there." The man pointed, Declan moving that way.

Standing in his office doorway, Declan froze once more. His eyes searched the room and he grew desperate, knowing that there wasn't anything that he could do at the moment. His mother was bound to a chair, a gag across her mouth. He could see the fear on her face. Next, he saw Eilis, also bound to a chair and gagged. Only she was angry. He could see that without hearing any words from her. Next to her, Naomi was also bound to a chair. How that happened, Declan had no idea. He could hear footsteps around him but his focus was on the three ladies. There was no sign of his father and the only thing that Declan could do was pray that he was out of the house and safe.

A shove to his shoulder sent him into the room. Declan stumbled as he tried to keep on his feet. Another shove sent him into his desk chair. The weapon was trained on him as he was bound.

What are they waiting for? That was a question he wanted an answer for. He was sure that would be answered at some point over the next little while.

Declan's gaze kept shifting between the man and the ladies. He frowned as he watched Eilis. Shewas up to something. Only he had no idea what that was. He was just afraid that she would be hurt.

The sound of the door opening and closing caught at their attention. Footsteps sounded on the wooden floor, heading their way. Declan drew in a deep breath, his eyes on Eilis. He could see the fear that flickered on her face before she shuttered it. Only her eyes seemed alive.

Angela watched the doorway, feeling her heart tighten with fear. The couple who had appeared in the doorway was not who she had expected. She caught the look on Declan's face and realized that he had expected them and that he was confident that these were the people who were after the couple.

Eilis watched the couple as well, their appearance confirming her suspicions. She had never felt comfortable around them. Only she had never known why. Now she had a good idea what they had been up to. She had been listening to the rumours on the street, the youths coming up to her over the last few days, talking with her, leaving notes, taking the money and food that she offered them. They had grinned as she thanked them, simply shrugging. They did what they needed to do, they said, just to keep their town safe.

"Well, well, well. Who do we have here?" The pompous voice of the man echoed loudly in the room. "Declan. Eilis. Just who we were hoping to see. The other two? Baggage that we'll get rid of as well." Jones Rogers strutted around the room, his heavy body making it difficult for him to do that. He loved his wine and rich food, and those had taken a toll on him.

His wife, Janie, simply stared at him and then at the four, a sneer on her face. She had no words for them. In fact, she looked down on them and always had. She had never needed to work and had decided that anyone who did work was worthless.

"What do you want, Rogers?" Declan found his voice, keeping it as neutral as he could. He knew that the man was standing behind him. He could see his mother looking that way every once in a while. Eilis on the other hand simply caught his gaze and then looked around.

Naomi despaired of doing what she knew best how to do, that was to get Eilis and Declan and Angela away. She had been outside on the back deck when the man had simply appeared, a weapon drawn and steady on her. She had had no choice but to return to the house. That had not been what she wanted to happen. Nor was this, to have the Rogers show up as they had. She knew that this meant their deaths, that the Rogers would not let them live.

With their attention on the Rogers, none of them heard the quiet opening of the door or the equally quiet footsteps heading their way. They didn't notice the shadows at the French doors. They had just decided that they had to find a way to free themselves and escape from the room.

"What do you want? You're in my house for a reason. So, start talking." Declan repeated himself, tensing as Rogers stopped in front of him. He was in pain and that was affecting how he reacted.

Rogers drew back a hand, the blow knocking Declan's head to one side. Declan's eyes closed from the pain even as he heard muted yelling from Eilis. He prayed that Eilis would be still. She would only bring the man's wrath on herself.

Rogers turned at hearing the muttering from Eilis. He strode to stand in front of her. A hand went out to grasp her hair, pulling her head backwards. She glared at him, not taking her eyes from his face. He frowned at her, suddenly uncertain as she was not acting as the others he had threatened did. He stepped back, almost into his wife.

Eilis kept glaring at him, praying that the sound she had heard was someone coming to rescue them and not someone on Rogers' side

"You will pay for that, little lady. You will not wake out of here alive. Nor will any of the others." Rogers shot a suddenly uncertain look at his wife. This was not going how they had planned and talked. These four were to be servile and cowed. Only they weren't and that puzzled him.

Janie Rogers found a chair to sit in. This would be entertaining, she decided. She knew that her husband would be the victor. She just liked seeing him win. And she had no doubt that he would. Neither one of them heard the footsteps creeping closer to the doorway.

Angela frowned, catching slight movement in the hallway. She breathed a prayer that it was someone to rescue them and not harm them. She studied each one in the room, taking hope from the determination in the other three captives. She prayed that they would survive and bring this couple, who had been the bane of many person's existence, to justice.

Frank watched closely, his mind racing as to the best way to proceed. He had to be careful. The man behind Declan, who he recognized as a hired assassin, would not hesitate to pull the trigger. And that put all four captives at risk. *Lord,* he prayed, *guide us here. Protect our friend. Help us to take these people down and bring them to justice.*

Chapter 41

Frank listened as Rogers began to boast, telling Declan and Eilis exactly why he had targeted them. He had not been aware of all what was going on but he had begun to dig below the surface. The work that Emma had done and that of Eilis' friends overnight had helped clear up the investigation to some extent. He had to prove what they had discovered but investigators were working on that. The scope of the investigation had grown to a level that none of them had expected.

"I don't get it, Rogers. Why us?" Declan was goading him, desperate to find out why Eilis had been on their radar.

"Why you?" Rogers' voice rose in anger and he almost stamped his feet in rage. "Why you? Why not you?"

"Yes, why us? Tell us. Why did you decide to go after us?" Declan was not backing down. There was too much at risk. And he felt that if he drew it out long enough, help would arrive. He didn't realize that help was there already and was listening in on the conversation.

"Why you? It's simple. You were there. That's how simple it was. We looked around for someone and you two won."

"Won what? Care to explain?" Declan's eyes were on Eilis, watching as her eyes moved to the doorway and then back to him. She was trying to tell him something, he realized. His eyes closed for a moment, praying that what she was signalling to him was true, that help was there.

"I would like to do that." The pompousness in his voice increased. "You two? You were just too goody goody. All your lives. Our son tried hard to be friends with you both but you rejected him. That drove him into crime."

Declan scoffed, waiting for another blow to land. It didn't, which surprised him.

"Really? I don't think so. There is more to this than that. We've heard the rumours over the years about you and your family. The bribes to government officials, the drug running, the human trafficking, the blackmail and extortion. How'm I doing?"

Rogers stared at him, spluttering in his inability to speak.

"That's not true. How can you say that?" Rogers had paled as Declan had spoken, confirming what he had said.

"Of course it is. We have proof of it which we passed on to the authorities. It's only a matter of time until they come for you. Are you planning on adding murder to the list? Or is that already on there?"

Declan kept his eyes on Eilis, seeing the very instance when her foot went out to trip Rogers. Rogers went down in a heavy fall, his breath knocked from him. Declan shoved his chair backwards into the man behind him, knocking him to the floor as well.

Frank moved in quickly as did the officers with him and those waiting outside the French doors. Shouts telling the three culprits not to move and that they were under arrest echoed through the room.

Watching as the three were handcuffed, read their rights, and then removed, Frank drew in a deep breath. He had been so afraid that it would go so wrong and one of the four would be killed. Officers moved in to free the four. Eilis found herself in Declan's arms, Angela's arms around them. Naomi moved away, searching for Richard and finding him outside waiting for her. He simply hugged her before turning her back to an officer who was waiting for her statement.

The other three on his team walked up to him, thankful that Naomi was safe as were the other three.

"Richard? It's over?" Timothy had to ask the question, sharing a look with the other two.

"It is, Timothy. It's over. They are safe and it's just the mopping up that needs to be done. We'll stick around for now. Just in case."

"Do we know that for sure?" Stephen was skeptical.

"We are, Stephen." Frank had stopped beside him. He had stepped away for the moment, to let others take the statements and then clear the rooms. The four would not be staying there that night, that much was obvious.

"I'm glad. This has taken enough from them all. We'll take them over to David and Angela. I spoke with Ashlynn. They're at the barricade. We'll just keep them there." Richard was thinking ahead. "We'll need to give you a couple of days to sort it all out."

"Thanks, Richard. That works. I'll come find you later." Frank walked away, fatigue washing over him. It had been a long few days, he thought. Now that the four young ladies were safe, maybe things would slow down. His footsteps stopped and he spun, searching for Ashlynn. He found her at the barricade, arms around her three girls, the three men standing grouped around her. She was intent on the house, watching for her youngest lady to appear. Frank began to pray for her, petitioning God to keep her safe. Somehow, this was not over for her, he decided. There was all that with the things that the young ladies had received. That had not been explained in any of their adventures, as they called them. He feared for his friend's life. Only time would tell if his fears would come true.

Angela walked out first, searching for David and then running for him, to be swept into his arms. Her sobs shook her body, the fear releasing in healing tears. He turned her away from the house, Timothy at his shoulder directing him to his vehicle and then away.

Declan waited for Eilis, simply reaching to wrap her close to him. She wasn't weeping, she was still too mad for that. It would come, he knew. And so would his tears. He had feared for both his mother's live and Eilis'. He didn't know how that they had managed to avoid death, but they had.

Frank walked through David's house late that night, not finding anyone up but Richard.

<hr>

"Richard? They're sleeping?"

"They are. The three ladies went home. They'll be back in the morning. Eilis and Declan are in the sunroom. They're not letting go of one another."

"Didn't think that they would." Frank reached to pour a cup of coffee, taking with thanks the plate of food handed him. He had not had time to eat much that day.

"It's really over?" Richard was hesitant to ask.

"It is. It is just as they guessed. All that. We have arrested those we needed to. People are beginning to speak with us, telling us just what all happened."

"I'm glad. Now those two can go on with their lives." Richard grew contemplative as he always did when a security assignment was ending. He could only praise God that the four had survived.

Epilogue

Turning from where he stood at the front of the church, Declan drew in his breath. Eilis moved towards him, her arm linked with her aunt, the long white gown and veil just showcasing her beauty. He was still amazed that she was his and loved him just as deeply as he loved her. He reached for her hand, a kiss dropped on Ashlynn's cheek. Their hands shook as they exchanged rings before they turned to be introduced to the friends and family gathered in the church.

Later that afternoon, Declan stood with the other three men, conversation light between them. He watched his beloved bride with her sister and cousins, laughing at something one of them had said. It had been so close, he knew, to losing her.

Ronan watched him before he shared a look with Gareth and Flynn. They knew somewhat how he felt.

"You're doing okay, Declan?" Flynn spoke for the three.

"I am, finally. I've been into counselling, which is helping. And talking with you three has helped." Declan drew in a deep breath. "I'm selling my house. We've bought another one."

"We wondered if you would. There are too many bad memories in that one." Gareth agreed with his sentiment.

———

Declan excused himself, moving towards his wife, finding her moving towards him. He simply wrapped her into his arms and kissed her.

"Okay, sweetheart?"

"Better than okay. And you?" Eilis grinned up at him, happiness radiating from her.

"I am. I was so afraid that I would lose you that last day. Has it been four months already?"

"It has been." Eilis hugged him. "I am so happy. I love you."

"And I love you." Declan turned as he felt a hand on his shoulder. "Mom? Dad?"

"Care to share your bride for a moment? We would like to hug her too." Angela laughed at her son before she swept Eilis into a hug. "I am so glad that you are a part of our family."

"You are? Who could tell?" Eilis hugged her back, laughing. The weight had been removed from her.

Frank had spoken with her that morning, just for a moment. He wanted to let her know that the trials were going ahead. They would need to testify, unless the group pled guilty. Declan and Eilis would willingly do that.

Declan walked away soon, Eilis' hand tight in his. They mingled with their friends and family, smiles on their faces. They were relaxed and knew that God had protected them. They were now ready to start on their adventure as newlyweds with God in control.

Ashlynn watched her youngest niece, standing where she was alone for the moment. She thought back over the years, watching in her mind Eilis growing from a terrified youngster suddenly orphaned to the confident glowing young bride. She was happy but sad as well. That portion of her life was now over and she could move on. Only she didn't know how to or where to.

Eilis appeared beside her at that moment, hugging her aunt.

"Thank you, Aunt Ash. You have been such a wonderful aunt and mother to me. I can't express how much God has blessed me with you. I love you."

"And I love you too. You are a beautiful, compassionate, Godly young lady. I am proud to be called your aunt. Now off with you two. Come see me when you get back." Ashlynn turned and walked away, leaving Eilis watching her, Declan's arms around his bride.

"She'll be okay, sweetheart. It's that her life is changing." Declan had had long talks with his aunt by marriage.

"It is. I wish Mom and Dad were here, but she has stepped in over time and become that mother to me."

Thank you for choosing the pick up the story of Eilis and her sweetheart, Declan. This is the last of the stories of the young ladies, leaving just their aunt's story to be told. Once more Eilis and Declan only shared the story as they felt the author could handle it. I never know ahead of time what will happen. Their characters decide to write the story.

This time, Abe and Emma didn't show up except to be mentioned, although Ian and Nathaniel did. Their story and their team's story is in the *His Guardians* series. Dave and Rylee's story is in *A Touch of His Garment*. Doug and Darci's story is *The Heart of a* Lion. Tag, Shea, and Evan's stories are in the *His* Dreamseekers series. Brownie's is in the *His* Searchers series. My characters just love to walk back and forth all the time. Usually there are more than just a couple show up.

I still have my Dad's cufflinks and tie tags from when I was a child. These are treasured memories of seeing him dressed up in a suit and tie for church, with cufflinks and tie tac in place.

The parable of the wise virgins has always been a favourite of mine. I can remember as a child hearing our pastor at the time preach a sermon on it. That has stuck with me. My father would often mention it. Dad was a carpenter but build furniture for me in his later years. He built me a stand for my keyboard, an organ stand that he called it. It has a high back with a music book rack, a roll top cover, storage on either end. I treasure it because it was something that he designed and created, a one of a kind piece. When he did it, he included some very precious things on it. On the back underneath the keyboard portion are seven pieces of wood. These he said were the seven churches in Revelations. On the top of the book rack, he carefully handcrafted what look like lamp chimneys. There are five. These he told me were the five wise virgins from the parable. Dad spent a lot of time in thought but never talked a lot about what he was discovering in Scripture. When he did, it was something like this. Dad graduated to heaven in 2012, about two and a half years after Mom. They are missed so very much.

Be the light out there for someone. We live in dark and dangerous times. Someone needs to see God shining through you. Keep your lamp polished.

God bless.

Ronna

www.ingramcontent.com/pod-product-compliance
Lightning Source LLC
Chambersburg PA
CBHW061253210726
48293CB00003B/943